Dear Reader,

Like the heroine of *Wanted: An Interesting Life*, I was once torn about how to live my life— staying in shared rooms at a student hostel or three-star hotel with blow-dryer? Tofu Surprise or big, expensive hunk of aged beef? I thought it would be fun to write about a young woman in a similar situation—someone trying to figure out who she is and who she belongs with. It's a premise rife with comic possibilities, so who better to publish it than Harlequin Flipside?

It's a thrill to be writing for a line devoted to romantic comedy, which I've discovered is my forte. I hope you enjoy reading *Wanted: An Interesting Life* as much as I enjoyed writing it.

And in case you're wondering, I eventually figured out that I didn't have to choose between Sylvia Plath and Jackie Collins— I could read both! In this spirit, you may want to pick up a volume of poetry when you're finished with this book.

Then again—nah! How 'bout another Flipside novel?

Fondly,

Bev Katz Rosenbaum

"I'm going to be capital-I Interesting for one night— see how it feels..."

Jake and Lou looked at the food their waitress placed on the table. The spinach in her salad was yellowish-brownish, and Jake's brown rice and lentil casserole looked like—

"Vomit," he said once the waitress had left. "It looks like vomit."

"It doesn't," Lou lied. "You're being a baby. It's probably fabulous. Try it. Did you expect the usual takeout stuff? We're in a new restaurant, trying new food."

With that, she took a deep breath and forced herself to put a piece of spinach in her mouth and chew.

"How is it?" he asked suspiciously.

"Tangy," she said when she had swallowed. It tasted as if the "chef" had poured half a gallon of white vinegar on the soon-to-be-rotten spinach. "Your turn."

He sighed. "Okay, okay." He shut his eyes as he took a spoonful of the mush. "Mmm. If the taste is any indication, I think our 'Interesting' new life isn't starting out so well...."

Wanted: An Interesting Life

Bev Katz Rosenbaum

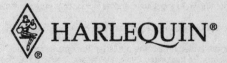

HARLEQUIN®

TORONTO • NEW YORK • LONDON
AMSTERDAM • PARIS • SYDNEY • HAMBURG
STOCKHOLM • ATHENS • TOKYO • MILAN • MADRID
PRAGUE • WARSAW • BUDAPEST • AUCKLAND

ISBN 0-373-44188-6

WANTED: AN INTERESTING LIFE

ABOUT THE AUTHOR

Bev Katz Rosenbaum is a former fiction and magazine editor. For three years she published *Slush*, a humor zine geared to aspiring authors. *Wanted: An Interesting Life* is Bev's second novel. She lives in Toronto with her husband, two children, an exceptionally needy canine and a large quantity of sea monkeys.

For Andie and Ricky Rosenbaum, the best kids in the world—to read when you're considerably older.

Huge thanks to all who helped out along the way, especially: Cary Fagan, Valerie Hayward, Wanda Ottewell, Susan Sheppard, Patricia Storms and, of course, Brian Rosenbaum.

A big shout out to the Slushies— subscribers and interviewees alike— whose hilarious and poignant stories provided much-needed encouragement and inspiration.

1

"LEMME GET this straight."

Lou Bergman shifted uncomfortably in her chair as Pauline Smith furrowed her brow. After Lou's horrific evening, she'd called an emergency meeting of her gal pals at their usual hangout—the Havajava Café on 56th Street—but she was starting to wish she hadn't.

Usually a Havajava rendezvous perked up Lou immensely. The Havajava was the kind of place that, had it existed anywhere but New York City, would have gone the way of the dodo bird after the advent of Starbucks. Its floors were made of beat-up wood, its walls were graced with wacky, cartoon-ish murals and there were funky, mismatched garden chairs for seats. Lou liked to think of it as the kind of place where the ever-narrowing segment of the population that still railed against the big chains could feel comfortable.

Not that it really was one of those places. The Havajava was, in fact, a big chain that very deliberately tried to attract the antichain contingent. It was owned by Jake Roth, Pauline's filthy-rich cousin. Hence, the use of the Havajava as the group's unofficial headquarters. Jake's office was upstairs.

Pauline looked at Lou sternly and said, "You purposely

picked your nose in front of your hyper-fastidious boy-friend Alan?"

Lou shrugged lamely.

"Lou, how could you?" cried Nicollete Lee, the third of their cozy troika. Nic was an innkeeper's daughter from rural upstate New York, complete with golden locks, bright blue eyes and a wardrobe that featured an alarming number of stewardess-style blazers. Lou found it hard to believe that Nic had been considered the crazy, artistic girl in her hometown secondary school. She was the star—well, the only—photographer at Harvey Gold Wedding Photography, and she and Lou—Harvey's videographer—were as different as Starbucks was from the Hava-java.

"Alan is the perfect catch!" Nic shook her head.

"The only people who regard Alan as the perfect catch are people who don't know him," Lou said defensively. "Do you know what it's like to have to go to the bathroom every single time you need to wipe your nose?"

"At least he was clean," Nic, ever the Pollyanna, ventured.

"Yeah, a clean *freak*, in the true sense of the word," Lou said firmly. "And *he* left *me*. Who can live like that?"

"So you just—reached in to bug him?" Nic said, uncomprehending.

"No pun intended," Pauline said, winking.

Nic looked at her blankly.

Pauline rolled her eyes. "Bug, booger? Never mind."

Lou sighed. "Of course I did it to bug him." She paused. "Okay, maybe I kind of lost it. But it seemed so unfair! I chose him because I thought he was too straitlaced to ever leave me."

Pauline rolled her eyes again. "Lou, I know you went into major panic mode when you turned twenty-nine last week, but you don't have to settle just because thirty's on the horizon."

"Yeah, and that's another thing. How could he leave me on my birthday?"

"It's not your birthday anymore," Nic said, patting her hand.

"Still," Lou muttered petulantly.

"What about that other guy?" Nic demanded. "The one you saw at the Dining Table after you ran out of the apartment?"

"You actually shop at the Dining Table?" Pauline asked incredulously. She'd come to the meeting late and had missed Lou's initial recap of her evening.

"Only for ice cream emergencies," Lou said, squirming. Generally she avoided the overpriced, upscale grocer that catered to West Side singles, as trips there required hours of preshopping grooming. "But c'mon, guys, it's at the bottom of my building. Gimme a break."

"I hope you at least forego the pasta salad," Pauline said firmly. "Seven bucks for a teensy container of macaroni you can boil yourself in, like, three minutes."

"But how do you get it to taste like that?" Nic asked seriously. "With all the oil and herbs and stuff?"

Pauline rolled her eyes yet again. "You add oil and herbs and stuff."

"It's never the same," Nic said wistfully. Being a rural innkeeper's daughter, she refused to buy prepared food as a matter of principle, but, oh, how she longed to.

"Back to that other guy..." Pauline tried to get the conversation on track again.

"I told you," Lou said, "Perry's artsy. He was disgusted to find out I made wedding videos."

"You're just assuming that."

"No, it was pretty clear. He actually laughed."

"I hate when they laugh," Pauline said.

"No one's ever laughed at *me* for being in the wedding business," Nic said.

"They have," Pauline said dryly. "You just didn't notice." She turned back to Lou. "So what does this Perry guy do?"

Lou sighed. "I was afraid to ask. But he was wearing clothes that scream 'cool career.' Naturally, *I* was wearing a stained sweat suit and my eyes were all red and swollen."

"Poor baby," Pauline said sympathetically, "you've had a rough night."

"You bet," Lou said mournfully. "In the space of one hour it was firmly established that I'm both a personal and a professional failure." She knew she was wallowing, but sometimes, she thought, a girl just had to wallow.

"Lou, no!" Nic reached across the table to grab her hands. "Alan is incredibly self-centered, and that other guy sounds pompous, too. What do you care what other people think?"

"I thought you liked Alan, and thought that I was too picky?" Lou said, exasperated.

"Lou, if you say Alan and Perry are bad men, I believe you." Nic spoke in a soothing tone, like a psychiatrist talking to a manic-depressive.

"Is Perry Moss related to Debbie Moss?" Pauline asked.

"Yeah. She's his sister. Why?"

"We're booked to do her wedding soon."

"You're kidding," Lou groaned. "I'm gonna have to become more interesting by then. What should I do?"

"You have to decide, once and for all, what you want to be when you grow up, kiddo," Pauline said.

Lou sighed. "I know, I know. It's the story of my life. I can't seem to find my niche. I'm no Steven Soderbergh, but

I'm not sure I can muster the enthusiasm required to film another wedding." Lou constantly defended her job at Harvey Gold Wedding Photography to her intellectual friends, but complained about it *ad nauseam* to her co-workers. "Maybe Rona Bernstein had the right idea after all."

"Who's Rona Bernstein?" Pauline asked.

"A childhood friend of mine." Lou smiled nostalgically. "We were pretty inseparable. Until high school. She became a vegan and started talking about living off the land. I thought she was nuts and stopped being friends with her."

"Do you know what happened to her?" Nic asked curiously.

"I lost touch with her, but I saw her mother a while back. Apparently she really is on a farm somewhere, being a vegan. And a quilter." Lou sighed again. "I never thought I'd end up envying Rona Bernstein."

"What makes Rona Bernstein happy isn't necessarily what's going to make you happy," Pauline commented.

"I know that, but at least she had the courage to do something capital-I Interesting. As opposed to taking a job her mother found her, like I did."

"Hear, hear," piped up Ingrid, one of the Havajava regulars sitting at the next table. All the regulars clustered around the front of the café, and frequently caught snippets of the conversations around them—and felt no qualms about joining in. It was one of the things Lou loved about the Havajava. It was also one of the things she hated about the Havajava.

Ingrid was a heavyset platinum-blonde who dressed eccentrically and was with a different, drop-dead gorgeous man every time they saw her. Today she was with a model-good-looking specimen who spoke like a matinee idol. It was one of life's little mysteries.

She raised her coffee cup and grinned at her companion. "To capital-I Interesting lives. And to getting rid of boyfriends who don't deserve us." She aimed a sympathetic smile at Lou. "You'll get over him, kiddo."

Lou sighed. "I know I will, Ingrid."

"You're very b-brave, w-wanting to change your l-life," Vanessa, another regular ventured. Vanessa was a timid brunette poet who usually sat in the corner.

"I second that emotion, Lou. You're an exceedingly cool chick," Zee, a wild-haired bike courier, added. He lifted his coffee cup. "Here's to the wild life."

"Here's to getting back on the road to finding Mr. Right," Lauren, a pampered twenty-something put in, glancing frostily at Zee.

"That boyfriend of yours probably didn't deserve you," Dent, a trucker, said.

"You'll get used to being alone," Sam, an unemployed, middle-aged nerd, complete with flood pants, put in.

"I—guess. Thanks for your support, everybody."

"By the way," said Ingrid, "this is Ted, everybody."

"Hi, Ted," everyone said. Zee began talking to Ted and everyone's attention shifted to that conversation.

"Hey!" Lou waved her hands in front of Nic's and Pauline's eyes. "Back to me, you two."

"How do you think she does it?" Nic asked, still looking at Ingrid, awed.

"I'm pretty sure she drugs them," Pauline said.

Nic's eyes widened. "Really?"

"No, not really!" Lou practically shouted while Pauline laughed. "She was joking, for God's sake. Now can we please go back to discussing my non-interesting life?"

"Lou, there are plenty of people who think videography is capital-I Interesting," Nic admonished.

"Sure, film festival documentaries," Lou said grumpily, "not wedding movies."

"Well, I think what we do is important," Nic said resolutely. "We make our living documenting milestones for people, reminding them of the love and the excitement they shared on their wedding day."

Lou snorted. "It's a good thing we edit out the screamfests and the catfights, then, isn't it? Honestly, Nic, how can you possibly remain a romantic while working in this business? Haven't you noticed that nothing kills love quite like organizing a wedding?"

Nic looked at her blankly. "I don't see that at all."

Lou turned to Pauline and said, "Once, after witnessing a particularly horrible and violent prewedding fight that ended with both parties vomiting on each other, this chick actually whispered 'Jitters' in my ear."

"It *was* jitters," Nic insisted. "They were sweet—like Sharon and Ozzie."

"Yeah, when he was still in his bat-eating stage," Lou said scoffingly. She shook her head. "Sorry, I've had it with propaganda. Not to mention those cheesy opening montages. I went to film school, for God's sake! Now look at me. I've sold out—become a total bore. God, it's all so frustrating. How did I get here? What am I doing on the West Side with all the other sellouts? Why aren't I living downtown?"

"Because you want to live in a nice, clean, spacious apartment," Nic said firmly.

"And how is it that I got together with Alan, a guy who's the sales director for a *tampon* manufacturer?"

It was a rhetorical question. She knew very well how. She'd been young and easily impressed. Alan was older, terrifically handsome and successful in the way she'd been raised to believe the word was defined.

"He was a creep," Pauline agreed.

Lou looked at her, surprised. "Did you think that all along?"

"Yup. I sure hope you don't get back with him now."

"Not a chance," Lou said firmly. "But why didn't you tell me?"

Pauline shrugged. "My opinion didn't matter."

Lou turned to Nic. "Nic, did you feel the same way?"

Nic sighed. "I never liked him."

Lou crossed her arms. "Well! Fine friends you are!"

"Oh, come on, Lou. That's a no-win situation for friends and you know it," said Pauline, shaking her head. "I shouldn't have said anything now, either. You'll be hurt that I disrespected your choice, even if it wasn't the choice you'd make now. I didn't mean to imply you made a lousy decision getting involved with Alan—"

"But that's just the thing—I *did* make a lousy decision getting involved with Alan," Lou cried. "That's *exactly* what I've been talking about. I've made a whole *bunch* of lousy decisions."

"Everyone's entitled to a questionable choice or two," Nic said, shrugging. "Even the heroines in the romance series I subscribe to. It's always there in the first chapter with the snakelike, soon-to-be ex-boyfriend."

"I could tell you a month's worth of stories about the terrible jobs I've taken and the louses I've become involved with," Ingrid interjected.

"We all make good choices and bad choices, Lou. That's life," added Pauline. "Relationship- and apartment-wise. Trust me, you'd get sick of the downtown scene pretty fast."

"Well, maybe through experience you've figured out

that this is the right area for you, but since I moved to the city, I've barely been south of 47th Street," Lou stated, "and I'm almost thirty years old. You know what?" She banged the table with her fist. "I need to make some major changes here. My life's a mess. It's gonna change."

"Hi, everybody. What's gonna change?" a deep, sexy voice said. It was Jake.

"Hi, Jake," the regulars all said in chorus, turning to look at him as they always did—as everybody always did.

He really was something to look at, Lou reflected, with broad shoulders, jet-black hair and a killer grin. And he perpetually looked as if he'd just stepped out of a magazine ad. Today, he was a Polo model in khakis and a light blue, button-down shirt. Generally his style of dress reflected his age—mid-thirties as opposed to Lou's own late twenties—as well as his financial status: well off, as opposed to, well, pathetic.

Which wasn't to say that Jake couldn't be as silly and immature as everybody else at times. He was always grinning and cracking jokes. He and Lou had always flirted with each other, but she'd never acted on the flirtation because of Alan. And she wasn't about to now, when she'd just made the decision to become capital-I Interesting and to stop dating guys like her ex whose only goals in life were to make enough money to keep their Saks-crazed girlfriends happy.

Jake pulled up a stool and leveled a gaze at Lou. "Pauline told me about—what happened. I'm sorry." He put his hand on Lou's, which caused a little *frisson* of… something…to snake up her spine.

He was about to say something else, but before he could Lou pulled her hand away and said, "Everyone's become just a little too tactile in the new millennium." She knew Jake was used to her gibes, but there was a look in his eyes she wanted to erase, so in a softer tone she added, "Thanks, Jake, but I'm fine, really. I seem to have temporarily lost my way, but I'm here to tell you I'm going on a quest." She was sure about it now.

"A quest?" Jake asked. "What sort of quest?"

Lou waved her hand. "An all-encompassing quest. I'm going to find out where I really belong—work-wise, apartment-wise, life-wise. No more settling or selling out."

"She's going to become capital-I Interesting," Nic said. "Like Rona Bernstein."

"Don't know her. So, what do you consider capital-I Interesting?" Jake asked curiously.

"Oh, you know, living somewhere that's really different, doing some kind of—interesting job..." She trailed off, realizing that she wasn't doing a very good job of expressing herself, possibly because she couldn't seem to visualize herself living anywhere but the upper West Side or working for anyone other than semiretired Harvey Gold....

JAKE TOOK A MOMENT to think before responding. He knew he had to be careful. This was an extremely important moment. He couldn't believe the opportunity that had dropped into his lap. Finally he was going to get a chance to prove to Lou that they belonged together. Of course, Alan had screwed things up royally—now she was going to bend over backward trying to find some artsy jerk—but Jake was pretty sure he could get her to realize who she belonged with—him!—eventually. He wasn't about to blow this. He'd never met anyone like Lou: gorgeous, funny and smart as hell—except when it came to Alan and, of course, this whole quest thing.

How to answer without ticking her off? He looked at her carefully and said, "You think you can draw lines like that—declare what's capital-I Interesting and what's not, who's a sellout and who's not? I know Alan was a scumbag, but what's wrong with wanting to make a little money? Personally, I think you'd hate the avant-garde, underground life."

Lou's eyes widened. *Damn*, he admonished himself. He'd gone too far. She was offended, thought he was lumping her in with all the other upper West Side girls....

Her response was cool. "Oh, really, Mr. Café Owner. Where did you get your philosophy degree? At business school?"

He smiled as an idea came to him. Maybe he could make this little argument work to his benefit.... "I've been on quests myself. I always ended up right back where I started from."

"Here at the Havajava? That's so depressing, Jake. People used to travel to places like Israel or India to reach a state of enlightenment. Now they get it at coffee chains."

He lifted his brows.

She sighed. "Sorry. That was mean."

"No problem. If you need to travel far and wide to seek answers, by all means, go. Far be it from me to discourage you."

"Hey, I get all my answers just travelling around the city," Zee said enthusiastically. "We live in the greatest city in the world! It's such an incredible microcosm. We have people from everywhere right in our own neighborhoods—it's amazing!"

Everyone looked at Zee for a moment.

"You're not from New York, are you?" Lou said.

"Me? Nope."

"I didn't think so." She turned back to Jake, who was still looking at her.

"Great haircut, by the way," he said.

"Thanks."

He continued to study her. She looked sensational, even in a worn tank top and threadbare sweats. She had a new short haircut—a sort of Audrey Hepburn-ish pixie thing. It was the last day of March and he guessed the cut had been a premature spring splurge.

"It's just that, to me, your life looks pretty good."

"You sound like my mother."

Okay, now she was identifying him with her parents—which definitely wasn't good. From the anecdotes he'd overheard, he knew that Estelle Bergman and her husband Freddy had been blessed with Lou late in life. Considerably older than her friends' parents and cautious—okay, crazy—by nature, Estelle and Freddy hadn't exactly encouraged risk-taking. They'd retired to Florida years ago, but still worried about Lou around the clock.

Lou shook her head. "No way am I falling into that trap. I've always listened to what other people told me. I've never listened to my own instincts."

"Also, I'll miss you if you quit hanging around here."

Lou paused for a moment, but she just said, "Damned if I'm going to keep hanging out in this joint. Jeez, it feels like we never go anywhere anymore. The Havajava uptown, the Havajava downtown. Don't get me wrong, Jake, I love the place, but who says we have to meet here every time? Who says we even have to meet for coffee all the time?"

Pauline and Nic looked horrified.

"What else would we drink?" Nic asked.

"I dunno—tea. Isn't it a big thing now?"

"I tried that bubble tea at a food fair a couple of weeks ago," Pauline said. "Damn near choked on one of those tapioca balls."

"Okay, fine, we'll stick to coffee. But let's try it with a meal, at least. There's a lunch place I heard about downtown called the Lost Llama. Why don't we meet there on a Saturday sometime?"

"You won't like it," Jake warned. "The coffee's terrible." He extended his hand. It was time to put his idea into action. It was perfect—he'd be able to spend tons of time with her while at the same time proving that they belonged together.... "I'll bet you ten free pounds of Colombian that in, say, one year, you'll decide that your job, the area you're currently living in and indeed, this coffee shop, are just about the most terrific places on earth."

Again, Lou hesitated for a moment. "And my personal life? Are you saying I'll be happy living out my days as an urban spinster?"

Jake cracked a small smile and paused a minute before saying, "I think you'll come to a pretty startling realization."

"Thus spake Nostradamus," she said, extending a hand to meet his. They shook.

She quickly withdrew her hand.

He raised his eyebrows.

"A year," she said.

"A year," he said.

"Okay," she said.

"Okay," he repeated.

It seemed anticlimactic to carry on the conversation after that, so the meeting broke up and Lou Bergman's quest for a whole new, capital-I Interesting life began.

2

April

BACK HOME, Lou vowed to buckle down and work on
Capra Girl, the screenplay she'd been working on sporadi-
cally. It was about Gigi Graham, a film snob who, bonked
on the head by a tape of *It's a Wonderful Life* at a video
store, suddenly begins to preach the gospel of hopefulness
and sentimentality to her irony-steeped friends.

If she wasn't going to work on the thing now, Lou
thought, when would she? She had a golden opportunity
here—a big chunk of time with no other obligations filling
it up—and it would be a crime to blow her chance. Not to
mention that she now had to prove to Jake Roth that she
was a capital-I Interesting person.

At her dining room table—okay, her Aunt Sukie's
bridge table, since Alan had taken the good one—she
closed her eyes, trying to visualize her heroine. Maybe that
was why she'd been stuck, she thought. She'd never really
had a clear picture of her heroine. Perhaps she needed to
really *know* Gigi—be able to instantly conjure up her image
and personality—before she could begin writing.

Lou had long imagined that Gigi was a short brunette.
She'd have glasses, too, she decided. Cool ones, with dark,
rectangular frames.

But Miss Intellectual would have to become perky after
viewing *It's a Wonderful Life* for the first time. Could a waif-

ish film snob look perky? Lou wondered. She could if she lost the glasses, she decided. And if she started wearing vintage print dresses. And ankle socks. And cute little loafers...

There. Pleased with herself, Lou decided that she was ready to write.

Very ready to write.

Except, no words were forthcoming.

Food, Lou decided. She definitely needed a snack. Her tummy was rumbling and she'd always been one of those people who had to be absolutely free of distractions before she could work.

In the kitchen she spent quite a bit of time creating the world's most gorgeous sandwich with sliced chicken, mayonnaise, tomato, lettuce and sprouts. When she finished the sandwich, it was off to the bathroom. The regular elimination of solids was an absolute must for one to work at one's peak condition.

Not to mention that it gave one a good excuse for reading *Vogue* cover to cover.

When she came out of the bathroom, she happened to notice what a mess her bedroom was. So, of course, she had to spend a good couple of hours reorganizing her closet.

And once that was done, she couldn't very well leave the spare bedroom a mess.

Or leave the laundry piled up in the laundry bin.

Or not clean the fridge.

Or the stove.

And of course, there were always shoes to shine and shirts to iron. Not to mention delicates to hand-wash, papers to file, photographs to organize in albums and letters to write...

Hours later, she decided she was too exhausted to work.

She'd start tomorrow, she decided. In the kitchen she made herself a cup of cocoa and flipped through some envelopes on the kitchen counter, opening a Visa bill.

Not three minutes later she was sitting at the bridge table in the dining room, the words pouring out of her as if they'd been waiting to come out for years. Necessity truly was the mother of invention, Lou mused as she pounded away at her keyboard.

She didn't know how long she'd been at her computer when she woke up. She vaguely remembered putting her head down on the keyboard midsentence. Yawning, she saved her work and shut the computer off. Wow! She was on page seventy-five of her first draft already—almost halfway through!

Exhausted, she dragged herself into the bathroom to brush her teeth, then hauled herself into her room to flop gratefully onto her bed and crawl under the covers.

She bolted upright when she saw a petite brunette perched on the footboard, filing her nails.

The brunette looked up and smiled. "Sorry, hon. I promise I'll clean up the mess."

"Who are you?" Lou said, pulling the covers up around her; she slept in the nude.

"I won't hurt you, silly. Don't you recognize me?"

The thing was, Lou did. It didn't seem like a dream, but apparently it was. The woman in front of her bore a startling resemblance to, well, herself. Except for the fact that she was wearing a 1940s-style print dress.

It was Gigi Graham, alias Capra Girl.

Lou pulled her blanket even more closely around her, partly because of modesty, but also because she never dreamed and Gigi, with her perky but ghostly smile, was creeping her out just a tad.

Gigi put her nail file down and smiled at Lou sympathetically. "Poor Lou. It's just a dream, hon."

"I gathered that," Lou said a little testily. "But why am I dreaming about *you*?"

Capra Girl smiled brightly. "I'm here to clear up this whole business with Jake, of course."

"What do you mean 'clear up'?" Lou asked a little defensively. Why was it, she thought, annoyed, that everyone in her life seemed to think they could handle her life better than she could?

Gigi shook her head. "Lou, Jake's a great catch. Everyone thinks so. It's so obvious the two of you should get together, but nobody wants to say anything for fear of upsetting you. That's partly why I'm here. Most people would be having this discussion with their best friends. In your case, things are extra complicated because Pauline is Jake's cousin and Nic is a little, well, dim. But you really have to reevaluate this whole quest thing, hon. It's all just a little misguided, to put it frankly. I guess I'm your...voice of reason, as it were."

"Whoa!" Lou said, shocked. "Wait a minute. I don't think you have any right to come in here and tell me what I should or shouldn't do—"

Gigi laughed a tinkly, otherworldly laugh. "I'm afraid neither of us can control when I appear or what I do."

Lou started to say something, then stopped. Gigi had a point. Lou couldn't very well discuss the bet—or her crazy attraction to Jake—with Pauline, since she was Jake's cousin. And much as she loved Nic, she didn't exactly respect her co-worker's advice in matters of, well, anything. Hashing things out with the dream figure might indeed be helpful.

"Okay," she found herself saying slowly. "I have many valid reasons for not wanting to get involved with Jake."

"Such as?"

Lou ticked off the points on her fingers, holding the blanket up around her by pressing her arms against it. "He's a businessman, which, by definition, means the bottom line is more important to him than anything else—"

"Debatable," Gigi said.

"It isn't," Lou insisted.

"You don't even know how much money he makes. And so what if he is ambitious and raking in the dough. Maybe he's amassing a fortune for his family and various causes," Gigi said, crossing her arms. "His parents, bless their dear, departed souls, were known philanthropists, after all. Jake has to have developed some charitable instincts along the way."

"Are you kidding? He's a playboy and I've never heard him mention any charitable endeavor." Lou felt guilty speaking badly about him, having just been reminded that his parents had both died years ago—one after another, each from cancer. Jake had been twenty—it was a couple of years before she'd met him through Pauline. He'd been on his own since then. It couldn't have been easy for him. She supposed he'd turned out all right, considering.

"You think he's a playboy?" Gigi asked, surprised.

"Yup. The kind that doesn't reveal details."

Gigi cocked an amused brow. "Isn't that good?"

"God, no! He's *too* secure in his masculinity. Those are the worst kind."

"I see," Gigi said, smiling. "Back to the charity thing. You really have no way of knowing what he's involved in."

"I'm sure I would have heard something at some point."

"Ever hear of Maimonides?"

"Mai—who?"

"Maimonides. Twelfth-century Jewish philosopher. Came up with the eight levels of charity."

Lou shook her head. When it came to spiritual education, Estelle and Freddy had gone for big holiday dinners over religious school. "Sorry," she said. "Doesn't ring a bell."

Gigi waved a hand. "In a nutshell, he said that the greatest level, above all, was to strengthen somebody's name by giving him a job."

Lou looked at her. "Your point?"

"Well, Jake employs an awful lot of people."

Lou cocked a brow. "That's the best you can do to sell Jake?"

"No. The level below that—the second best level of charity—is giving without a lot of fanfare. The idea is, the donor shouldn't know who's getting the gift and the recipient shouldn't know who the donor is."

"Again, I seem to be missing something."

Gigi shrugged. "Just because Jake refuses to splash his name all over the society pages doesn't mean he's not doing good works."

Lou considered this. "It's a possibility, but pretty far-fetched, I'd say. Jake loves a party, loves the action."

"He's socially well-adjusted, but he's not a creep. There's a difference."

"I never said he was a creep," Lou protested.

Gigi leaned forward even more. "Lou, life's too short to be cynical. Love is love." She appeared to think for a moment. "You know, the character of Capra Girl in your screenplay represents your innermost desires."

Lou started to protest, but stopped. Was Gigi right?

The dream figure shook her head and smiled. "What makes you think you're cut out to be a radical, anyway?"

"I never said I was a radical," Lou protested. "But I *can* be rebellious."

Gigi waved a hand. "Semantics. Radical, rebel, free spirit. I repeat my question. What makes you think you're a *rebel?*"

Lou thought for a moment. "I sleep in the nude!" It was all she could think of.

Gigi looked at her and crossed her arms. "Let's talk about sex."

"Excuse me?"

"You heard me. Sex. S-e-x. Are you getting any?"

Lou pulled herself up stiffly. "I had a very healthy sex life with Alan, thank you very much."

"And now that that's over?"

"I don't believe I wish to discuss my sex life with you," Lou said primly.

"Ha! That's because you don't have one! You're an old-fashioned girl, Lou. You need to be in love to have sex."

"What's wrong with that?" Lou asked a little huffily.

"Nothing's wrong with that! That's what I'm trying to tell you! You're an old-fashioned girl—you need a man you really connect with."

"Right. And who's to say there isn't some great, artsy guy out there who I'm really going to connect with?"

Gigi sighed. "Lou, do you or do you not feel tingly all over when Jake Roth touches you—looks at you?"

Lou looked away. "Sure, there's a smidgen of attraction. There's a smidgen of attraction with a lot of guys."

"Is there?" Gigi began to pace like a courtroom lawyer. "Let's talk about your romantic history."

"Let's not," Lou muttered.

Gigi stopped and looked at her. "Not much to tell, is there?"

Lou threw up her hands, then promptly brought them

down again to catch the falling blanket. "No, there isn't. That's the trouble! I'm finally trying to change things!"

"Lou, honey," Capra Girl said in a soothing tone. "You're twenty-nine years old."

"Exactly!

"Haven't you ever heard the saying 'You can't teach an old dog new tricks'?"

Lou looked at her. "Did you just call me an old dog?"

Gigi sighed. "Sweetie pie, you can't force these things. Your romantic history is what it is because you connected with only a handful of guys. If you were going to be all rebellious and experimental, you would have been that way long before now."

"But the way I grew up—"

"Honeybunch, I'm sure plenty of Long Island girls have belts full of notches."

Lou couldn't argue with that. She could name a dozen girls off the top of her head who had slept with more men than Rock Hudson.

Still, she felt the need to protest again. "I dated plenty of guys in high school," she said.

"Right. All disasters." Gigi struck a finger. "Arnold Klein."

"Okay, that *was* a disaster, but only because—"

"Marvin Brown."

"He had this very odd smell—"

"Nicky Friedland."

"Didn't read enough."

"Paul Cohen."

"His hair was too curly."

"Jerry Sherman."

"His was too straight."

"Billy Eckler."

"He bit his nails. He was always putting these bloody

stumps on my shoulder." Lou shuddered. "It was like a horror movie."

Gigi rolled her eyes. "Ron Schindler."

"Cracked his knuckles. Drove me crazy."

Gigi lifted a brow. "You broke up with him because he cracked his knuckles?"

Lou crossed her arms defensively. "If there are things that bother you about a person, it's better to end the relationship than drag it on until you're married with children."

"Right you are. But my point is that you didn't ever say to yourself, 'Well, I'm not going to marry this guy, but I might as well have a little fun.'"

Lou shifted uncomfortably on the bed. "No, I've never been able to do that."

"Exactly! Face it, Lou, you're simply not rebellious or experimental by nature. Only two men have brought out the wild woman in you."

"Jon and Dex," she murmured. She'd met both at NYU, though neither had been in film. Jon had been premed; Dex, prelaw. Jon had broken her heart when he'd gone off to England and Dex, whom she'd taken up with soon afterward, eventually decided to settle in California. She hadn't considered going with either of them—though both had asked. She hadn't wanted to leave New York and she'd assumed—wrongly—that the world was populated with many more Jons and Dexes.

"Right. Sexy, interesting guys with big hearts and good heads on their shoulders. Not unlike—"

Lou rolled her eyes. "Don't even say—"

"Jake," Gigi said triumphantly.

"You haven't mentioned Alan."

Gigi cocked her head. "Why did you go out with him, anyway?"

Lou sighed. "Because he's gorgeous. There was an attraction there, and even though he did stuff that bugged me, I thought I might as well try to develop a relationship with that kind of guy—the kind of guy everyone in my family wanted me to be with." She looked at Gigi. "Jake isn't any different from Alan—that's *my* point. He's just another businessman with money."

"Lou, Jake thinks. And he has a good heart. He's not like those guys. He's not the next Alan. He's the next Dex."

"I'm not at all sure about that, but even if you're right, I'm trying to figure out my career here, too. This isn't just a man thing. I don't think it's the best time to get involved with anyone right now."

Gigi perched at the end of Lou's bed. "You know, I've never understood that argument. Who says you can't have a fulfilling personal life at the same time as a fulfilling professional life? It's so easy with the right person. You help each other."

"And you know this from personal experience?" Lou asked sarcastically. "Do people get married in dreamworld?"

Gigi smiled. "Of course they do! And as far as career risks go, sweetie, you've blown several great opportunities already. If you'd gone with Jon to England, you could have made documentaries for the BBC. If you'd followed Dex to California, you could have been a famous feature film director by now!"

"That's exactly what I'm trying to say," Lou said, exasperated. "I know I've played it safe. I don't *want* to play it safe anymore. Don't you think I know how easy it would be to fall into a relationship with Jake? Or to stay at Harvey Gold for the rest of my life?"

Gigi came over and put her hands on Lou's shoulders. "Oh, honey, don't you see? You're not playing it safe—

you're following your heart's desire—doing what comes instinctively."

Lou sighed. "Look, all I'm trying to say is that it's more complicated than you think."

"No, it's less complicated than *you* think."

It was eerie how much Gigi sounded like Jake, Lou thought.

She shrugged. "We'll just have to agree to disagree."

Gigi shrugged back elegantly. "Okay, but I warn you, until you see the light, you're going to be hearing a lot from me during this pre-midlife crisis or whatever it is you're going through."

Great, Lou thought as her phone lit up with her mother Estelle's number. *Another female haunting my daily life....*

3

JAKE GRINNED AT HIMSELF as he looked in the mirror. Tonight he'd make his first move. He'd been clever about it—waiting two whole months after making the bet with Lou before doing it. But he'd decided the last thing he wanted to do was to rush her. Rushing was always foolish. Good things came to those who waited. He was prepared to wait the whole year, if necessary. He looked in the mirror once again and adjusted his beret. He looked ridiculous. It was all part of the plan....

LOU ANSWERED THE DOOR to find Jake dressed for Halloween in black pants, a black turtleneck shirt, black beret, checked jacket and an ivory scarf flung around his neck.

"Aren't you going to ask me in?" he said after a moment, grinning widely.

No, she thought, panicking. He'd never seen her apartment and that was fine by her. It had been Alan's and she'd never even protested the all-taupe decor. And, once again, she'd been caught in sweatpants, without a stitch of makeup on her face, by a great-looking guy standing less than six inches away from her. Despite his weird outfit, he looked sensational.

Which was another reason she didn't want to let him in. She was afraid she'd pull him onto the sofa the moment he stepped over the threshold and ravish him right then and there.

Not that he was the kind of guy she wanted anymore, she told herself for the umpteenth time since her breakup with Alan.

"Earth to Lou."

She snapped out of her reverie. "What? Oh..." She looked at him and crossed her arms. "Aren't you supposed to say 'Trick or treat'?"

He spread his arms out. "What? You don't like it?"

Sighing, she opened the door wider to let him in. "Would you please explain what you're up to?" She narrowed her eyes. "And how did you get my address?"

"Pauline, of course. And I'm here because we're going to a spoken word performance. In—" he looked at his watch "—about fifteen minutes, so you'd better hop to it." He strode over to the couch and took a seat, crossing one leg over the other nonchalantly.

She shut the door and crossed her arms. "Excuse me? I thought you said we're going to a spoken word performance. But I must have heard wrong."

"Nope, you heard right. I'm going to be capital-I Interesting for one night—see how it feels."

Lou was tempted momentarily. Anything to take her mind off the dreams she'd been having and the voices she'd been hearing. And the fact that, just earlier, she'd notified Harvey Gold of her impending resignation. *You have a nest egg*, she reminded herself for the hundredth time since her meeting with Harvey. That nest egg would support her until she finished her screenplay.

Still, she couldn't possibly go out with Jake.

"Very funny. Ha, ha. Okay, you've had your laugh. Now you can go home." She opened the door again and held it ajar.

"Lou, I'm serious." He made a hangdog face. "It'll be fun. C'mon. Show me how the other half lives. And don't you need to get out? Pauline told me you just quit your job. You don't want to sit here worrying if you've made the right decision all night." He held up a pair of tickets. "Please?"

She moved closer to the couch and crossed her arms again. "Why?" she asked suspiciously.

"Why what?"

"Why are you here? Why did you get the tickets?"

"Because I want to spend an evening with you. And because it will be fun. And because friends should do stuff together."

"Is that what we are?" she asked tentatively. "Friends?"

He looked her in the eye. "Sure we're friends. Aren't we?"

She looked away. "And you think a friend can just pop in anytime and expect the other friend to drop everything?"

"I asked Pauline if you were busy. She said you weren't."

Damn. Lou was sure Jake didn't treat his dates this way. He probably gave them a week's notice so they could buy new wardrobes for their meals at Moomba.

Not that she wanted to be anything more than friends with Jake Roth, she said to herself once again.

She sighed. "Give me five minutes."

He grinned. "Deal."

Five minutes later she emerged from her bedroom wearing jeans and a black T-shirt—no scarf or beret. "You know," she said, "this may come as a huge shock, but today's literary types don't dress like beatniks. The times, they have a-changed."

He stood. "Wow, you look great."

She tried to hide her pleasure. "Yeah, well, you're lucky I agreed to be seen with you in that getup."

"C'mon, lemme have some fun."

"You're really going to wear that?"

"I didn't bring any other clothes." As if noticing her place for the first time, he suddenly looked around and said, "Hey, this isn't bad."

She wrinkled her nose. "It's a wannabe apartment."

He lifted a brow. "A wannabe apartment? What does it want to be?"

She shrugged. "A bigger, classier place—on the upper East Side."

"Ah."

"I probably won't be here much longer. Besides the fact that I hate it, I can't afford it. And I don't particularly want to get a roommate."

"Right. Well, shall we?" He gestured toward the door.

"Lead the way, and try not to embarrass me too much."

She hoped her nonchalant attitude was a good cover for the surprising and sudden nervousness she felt, complete with jumping heart and butterflies in her stomach. Friends or not, this was the first time they'd been out alone together and it definitely felt...odd.

As they went down the elevator, she tried not to let him see her inhale his delicious scent—CK? Polo?

Stop it, she told herself once they were in his car—an Audi with buttery-soft leather seats. She nearly groaned with pleasure. She took the subway everywhere and, while she didn't use to mind, lately the whole public transportation thing had begun to wear on her. On her last subway ride she'd been sandwiched between two rap fans wearing sound-leaking Walkmans and had taken note of about a dozen suspicious-looking characters on the platform before boarding. She'd expended so much energy keeping herself pressed firmly up against the wall that she'd had none left with which to reprimand the sound-polluting music lovers once in the subway car.

She closed her eyes. What would it be like to be driven places in a vehicle like this every day?

Stop it! He's made it perfectly clear that you're just friends.

And she didn't want to be anything more.

Despite the fact that he was the most fabulous-looking friend she'd ever had. Even in that ridiculous outfit, he looked like the world's most eligible bachelor. And he was fun, to boot.

She sighed and repeated the mantra in her head. *I am just friends with Jake Roth, I am just friends with Jake Roth....*

"So, when was the last time you went to a poetry reading?" he asked as he pulled the car onto the street.

"High school. I loved it. Don't know why I haven't been since."

"Well, then, aren't you glad I came along?"

She refrained from answering.

"I can't believe I gave up that parking spot in front of your building. Did you see that spot?"

"It was a great spot," she agreed. "You got lucky."

"A spot like that makes you want to just keep the car parked."

Lou laughed. "And what? Not go out? Take the subway? Kind of defeats the purpose of having a car, doesn't it?"

He laughed back—a deep, rich sound that did alarming things to Lou's insides. "It does. But, you know, I know a guy who knows a guy who's famous for just finding great parking spots and reading the paper in his car."

"I know a guy who knows a guy.... I smell an urban myth."

He laughed again.

"Why don't you use a car service in the city?" Lou asked, curious. "Surely it's less of a hassle than driving and parking in Manhattan."

He threw her a sidelong glance as he took a corner. "A car service—yuck!" He feigned a British accent. "To Yankee Stadium, James."

Lou laughed. "Point taken."

They drove the rest of the way in companionable silence.

Finally, Jake said, "Here we are." He pulled neatly into a spot in front of the Sacred Squash, a vegetarian restaurant-café.

"Another great parking spot," Lou commented.

As Jake straightened his wheels, he glanced out the window and said, "Not difficult in this neighborhood."

They'd gone east—so far east they were almost in the river, Lou thought. Before she could open her door, he was there doing it for her. *"Après vous, mademoiselle."*

"Thanks." She took in a sharp breath. Why did he look...different? She couldn't breathe for a moment. He had left the beret, jacket and scarf in the car. Clad only in the black pants and turtleneck shirt, he looked like a model—no, a movie star.

He grinned. "You didn't think I was actually going to wear all that stuff inside, did you?"

"Of course not." She started walking.

"You did, didn't you?"

"Did not."

"Did, too." He opened the door to the restaurant for her.

They were the only ones there, save for a lone table of two. An extremely thin and pale young woman took their tickets and led them to a table.

"Not very busy," Lou commented when the waitress had left.

"Hmm, wonder why," Jake answered, peering at the menu the waitress had handed him. "Could it be the wilted flowers, the smell of mushrooms gone bad, the atmosphere of sad desperation?"

The place *was* depressing, Lou thought, with dirty pea-green walls and tables that looked as though hordes of termites might pop out of them at any moment. But she was damned if she was going to let Jake know what she really thought. "If you're just going to make fun," she said primly, "I'm leaving."

"I won't say another word. You're right. I shouldn't make fun. Who knows? Maybe they'll surprise me with their culinary expertise and the brilliant live performances. Tell me you haven't eaten dinner."

"I haven't," Lou admitted.

"Great. What looks good?"

Lou glanced at the menu. *Nothing,* she thought. There was a lot of brown-rice-based stuff. It seemed she'd been wrong when she'd told Jake that the literati had changed. The menu here was definitely stuck in the 1970s. She was reminded of her cousin Ellen, who had been a hippie and still served rice and lentil casseroles for dinner.

"I'll just have a spinach salad and an Earl Grey tea," she said after a while.

"You sure? You don't strike me as the salad type."

"What does that mean?"

"Nothing bad. Only that I've gone out with too many girls who don't eat. Their appetites in other departments are similarly uninspired."

Lou's heart started to pound. She fought to steady its rhythm and say as casually as she could, "We're not 'out.' We're just friends, remember?"

"Ah, yes. How could I forget?"

Just then the waitress—the same frightened-looking

creature who'd led them to their table—came to take their orders.

"My companion," said Jake, winking at her, "will have a spinach salad and an Earl Grey tea, and I'll have the brown rice and lentil loaf and a glass of dealcoholized white wine."

Lou almost sunk into the floor. Jake frequented the finest restaurants and drank the best wines. Though why *she* felt embarrassed, she had no idea—it had been his idea to come!

"Good choice." The waitress smiled wanly. He smiled back. God, he was something, Lou thought, swallowing hard. *I am just friends with Jake Roth. I am just friends with Jake Roth...*

"Penny for your thoughts," he said once the waitress had gone.

"I was just thinking about how, um, I'm looking forward to hearing the poems."

"Are you a big poetry reader?"

"Well, no, not exactly. I try to keep up with current novels, though. A lot of the best novelists are poets, too. They really know what to do with...words."

Pretty soon, with her lame conversation, he wouldn't even want to be her friend, she thought.

"I've been trying to read more." He mentioned a novel that had been getting a lot of buzz and asked if she'd read it.

"Um, no, I haven't. But I've been meaning to."

He mentioned another one.

"Haven't gotten to that one, either."

"You're surprised, aren't you?"

"Surprised? Why would I be surprised?"

"That I actually read. You didn't expect it."

"That's not true," she lied. In point of fact, she was ex-

tremely impressed. Most other sellouts-shallow material-
ists she knew didn't read, except for stock market reports
and quarterly reviews.

He grinned. "I like that I surprised you."

She wasn't sure how she felt about being surprised.

A couple of people came into the restaurant. The woman
looked familiar, but Lou couldn't place her. She was on the
plump side and her head was an unruly tangle of dark
curls. She looked annoyingly serene.

"Do you know her?" Jake asked, following Lou's glance.

Just then Lou realized who it was. The mystery woman
was none other than Rona Bernstein—the vegan who'd
been hurt when Lou had broken off their friendship.

"No," Lou lied. If she'd said yes, Jake would have urged
her to say hello. Rona would have been frosty and Lou
would have ended up telling the whole story to Jake, who
would have laughed his head off upon finding out that
Lou had once broken off a friendship with someone just
because she'd become capital-I Interesting.

She hoped Rona didn't see her. Avoiding her gaze was
going to be difficult in a small, empty restaurant....

She moved her chair slightly and hunched a bit.

"Is something wrong?" Jake asked.

"No, nothing. Backdraft," she said.

"Backdraft?"

"A draft on my back. Don't worry about it. I'm fine
now."

Luckily she was saved from any further inane conversation by the waitress, who set their meals down on the table.

They just looked for a moment. The spinach in Lou's
salad was yellowish-brownish in color and Jake's brown
rice and lentil casserole looked like—

"Vomit," he said once the waitress had left. "It looks like vomit."

"It doesn't," Lou lied. "You're being a baby. It's probably fabulous. Try it."

"Do I have to eat my vegetables, too?" He stared forlornly at the sad, wilted green beans lying beside the pile of brown rice and lentil mush.

Lou looked at his vegetables. "No," she said. She couldn't expect miracles. "Would you like to share my spinach salad?" she offered graciously.

"That's some choice," he said glumly.

"I guess that's a no," she said. She took a deep breath and speared a spinach leaf with her fork. She forced herself to put it in her mouth and chew.

"How is it?" he asked suspiciously.

"Tangy," she said when she had swallowed. Which was the understatement of the century. It tasted as if the "chef" had poured about a half a gallon of white vinegar on the soon-to-be-rotten spinach. "Your turn."

"I don't think I can do it," he said in a grim tone.

"Come on, a worldwide traveler like yourself afraid of a little experimentation? What do you do when you're on some exotic island? Look for a McDonald's?"

He sighed. "Okay, okay." He shut his eyes as he fed himself a spoon of the mush. "Mmm, tastes as good as it looks."

Lou couldn't help but smile. And the smile led to a laugh and the laugh led to a giggle. Jake joined in with great, big, booming laughter. Soon, tears were running down their faces.

"Is—everything okay?" The waitress had materialized at their table. She looked scared.

"Perfect," Jake gasped. "I noticed you had ice cream for dessert. Can we have some of that?"

"Sure. I'll bring it when you're done."

"Oh, I think you can bring it now. We sort of overestimated how much we could put away here."

"Oh. Are you sure you want dessert, then?"

"Bring it on." He smiled widely. "One must always leave room for dessert."

The waitress smiled. Jake Roth had worked his magic. Lou had to hand it to him. Alan would have thrown a hissy fit and sent his food back.

The ice cream, thankfully, tasted like any other ice cream. Lou had suspected they'd try to make it without cream or sugar. But it was delicious. And it had been made on the premises, the waitress informed them proudly when they were done.

While they'd been eating dessert, a few other people had trickled in. Lou noticed they all ordered beverages, but no food.

"I don't think I needed to order the tickets in advance," Jake said dryly.

"I wonder why they even bother with tickets?" Lou said.

"Gives 'em something to do," Jake said.

Soon the lights dimmed and the waitress came on "stage"—a small, slightly raised platform at one end of the room that barely qualified for the name—and said, "Thank you all for coming tonight. It's our spoken word performance evening here at the Sacred Squash and so, without further ado, I'd like to welcome Michelle Proust, our first performer, with whom you will no doubt be familiar from her work in *Words and Windows*, the well-known art and literature journal."

"Do you know it well?" Jake whispered to Lou.

"Never heard of it," she whispered back.

"Ladies and gentlemen, Michelle Proust."

There was a smattering of applause as a youngish woman with jet-black hair and kohl-rimmed eyes took the stage.

On second thought, Lou mused, she wasn't so young-ish. The long hair had fooled her. She was decidedly mid-dle-aged.

She glared at Lou and Jake, and began to speak.

"I am alone, weeping, weeping.
  I am alone, creeping, creeping.
  I am alone, steeping, steeping
  In the tea of my anger."

Lou nearly erupted in giggles again and forced herself not to look at Jake. She knew Michelle wasn't finished yet.

"I am but a fragile flower,
  Drying, drying,
  Dying, dying,
  Under the hot sun of
  Your contempt."

With that, Michelle threw herself onto the floor, curled up into a fetal position and let out the loudest wail Lou had ever heard. She wondered if the poet was in psychother-apy.

Perhaps she *needed* to be in psychotherapy, Lou thought.

As suddenly as it had begun, the wail stopped. Lou was just about to applaud politely when Michelle sprang up and shouted,

"You are but a lying, lying,
  Cheating, cheating,
  Man. And I
  hate you!"

She sank down onto the floor again, weeping softly.

"Do you think she's really crying?" Lou asked Jake wor-riedly.

"I don't think so," he whispered. "Look, she's up again."

Indeed, she was smiling and nodding. A few people clapped halfheartedly. Lou and Jake joined in.

"Well, what did you think?" Jake asked Lou when Michelle had exited the stage. He talked quietly, because Michelle had sat at a nearby table, there being nowhere else for her to go.

"It was very...interesting," Lou said diplomatically.

"Interesting," Jake said, crossing his arms.

"Yes. I find it fascinating that some people can put their emotions right out there like that. I think we can all learn from performances like Michelle's."

He looked at her closely. "You do."

She couldn't respond because the waitress-emcee was introducing the next performer.

"Thank you, ladies and gentlemen. And thank you, Michelle. Your performance was truly inspirational." Her eyes filled with tears. "I, for one, learned a great deal from it. I realized that I can no longer let my anger eat me up inside. I have to let it out and—"

She seemed to realize where she was and cleared her throat. "Now, then, we have another performer I'm sure you'll welcome generously—Gerald McGibbon. Gerald is a regular performer here at the Sacred Squash. He has made a CD of his spoken word art—"

"When did they stop calling it poetry, anyway?" Jake whispered.

"—that we have available for purchase at the cash register. If you like Gerald's work, please support his art. And now, put your hands together for Gerald McGibbon."

"Suddenly she thinks she's a talk show host," Jake muttered. Lou shushed him.

Gerald began speaking in a monotone:

"Tables. Chairs. Floors. Walls. Roofs. People. Dogs. Cats. Horses. Pain.

Books. Records. Clocks. Jars. Windows. Refrigerators. Stoves. Pain.

Computers. Sweaters. Paper. Pencils. Fixtures. Microwaves. Pain.

Pain. Pain."

He bowed his head. Once more there was a smattering of applause. He spoke again when it died down.

"I. Am. In—" he, like Michelle, sank to the floor "—Pain."

"He thinks *he's* in pain," Jake whispered as he clapped. Lou smiled.

Gerald joined Michelle at the nearby table. Lou could hear snippets of their conversation.

"You stole my sinking-onto-the-floor move," Michelle was saying accusingly.

"You can't copyright a *move*, Michelle," Gerald said.

"You can't copyright anything," Michelle retorted. "You couldn't even get *Words and Windows* to publish your stuff. You made that CD in your basement."

"So what if I did. It's guerilla art."

"More like art made by gorillas."

"C'mon, let's blow this Popsicle stand," Jake said to Lou, grinning as he threw an assortment of bills down on the table.

She didn't have to be asked twice.

On the way out, she bumped into Rona.

"Lou? Lou Bergman?" Rona said.

"Rona! Hi! Wow, it's—great to see you! How are you doing?" Lou hoped her enthusiasm would dissuade Rona from being frosty.

Rona was not frosty. She did, however, look amused, which bothered Lou even more. "I'm doing great. And you?"

"Terrific. Oh, Rona, this is Jake, a good friend of mine."

Jake extended his hand. "Nice to meet you."

She shook his hand warmly. "Likewise."

"So, Lou, I hear you've been working for Harvey Gold."

"Not anymore," Jake said. "She just quit. She wants to become an avant-garde filmmaker."

"Really," Rona said, lifting her eyebrows. "Isn't life ironic?"

"Just like Alanis Morissette says," Lou said brightly, grabbing Jake's elbow and dragging him toward the door. "We have to go. It was great seeing you again, Rona. I hear you're doing great with your quilts. Well done. See you later."

She practically pushed Jake out of the restaurant and toward his car.

"So what was all that about back there?" he asked when they were almost home and had finally run out of small talk.

"What was all what about?" Lou asked, feigning ignorance.

"That business with that woman—Rona. Didn't Nic mention her name a while back?"

"Possibly. Rona's an old friend."

He cast a sideways glance at her. "An old friend?"

"That's what I said."

"That's it?"

"Yup."

"She's more than just an old friend," Jake said. "You're hiding something."

"I'm hiding something? I don't hide things. I'm not a game player." Which was generally true.

"You're not, huh?" He looked at her intently.

Disconcerted, she said, "So what do you think of those Yankees?"

He laughed. "Forget about the Yankees. What did you think about tonight?"

"I already told you. I admire those people."

"You thought their stuff was good?"

Lou shrugged. She couldn't very well tell him the truth. That she'd hated it—that she'd hated poetry since reciting "Jack Frost" at an assembly in second grade. She'd thrown up on stage. "I don't know much about poetry. I'll admit it's really not my thing."

"And the food? You like what capital-I Interesting people eat?"

"Not all Interesting people eat like that," Lou said. At least, she hoped not.

"You won't admit it, will you?"

"Admit what?"

"That you're just not a capital-I Interesting person at heart. No offense."

She stiffened. "How do you know what I am at heart?"

He shot her an intense sidelong glance. "I think I have a pretty good idea. You're a homebody. You like staying close to friends and family. You dislike pretentiousness. You need security, loyalty...love." Jake paused. "You're an extremely interesting person, Lou, just not a capital-I Interesting person." He smiled. "And I much prefer the small-i kind."

Her heart skipped a beat.

Just then, they arrived in front of her building.

"Is that why you took me tonight?" she asked slowly. "You suspected I would hate it and you wanted to make a point?"

He smiled. "Something like that."

"You know, Jake, I could have just as easily taken you to one of those yuppified steakhouses and made a similar point."

"Oh, yeah?"

"Yeah."

He extended his hand. "It's a deal."

"What?"

"I accept the challenge. You decide when and where. Take me somewhere you think I'd like to hang out and prove that *my* lifestyle is ridiculous."

"That's silly. I'm not going to—"

"Scared?"

She glared at him.

He grinned. "C'mon. Do it." He was still holding out his hand.

She sighed and shook his hand. "Deal."

She tried to extract her hand after a moment, wanting to get rid of the sudden, alarming tingling she felt all over her body and the urge she had to curl up against him.

She managed to pull away, finally. "Well, thanks. And good night."

He smiled. "You're not going to ask me up?"

"I thought we were just friends."

"Ah, yes. Friends."

"So good night."

"Good night," he said silkily.

Her knees almost buckled as she exited the car.

"WELL, THAT WAS CERTAINLY capital-I Interesting," Gigi Graham, alias Capra Girl, said much later once Lou was in dreamland. Lou had expected her. She always showed up to say "I told you so." "Do you have anything you want to tell me?"

"Only that I really wish you'd stop putting your nose in where it doesn't belong," Lou said petulantly.

"Is that what you think I'm doing? Remember, Lou, the Gigi Graham of *Capra Girl* expresses your innermost wishes."

"You don't think I'm capable of creating a character who thinks differently than I do?"

Gigi put her nail file down on the windowsill beside Lou's bed and crossed her arms. "Lou, have you ever wondered why you have this affinity with Frank Capra?"

"I like his movies," Lou said, not wanting to prolong the conversation.

"He's not exactly dark," Gigi commented. "He's sort of the antithesis of capital-I Interesting, don't you think?"

"Capra can be dark," Lou protested. "What about that scene in *It's a Wonderful Life* when George almost jumps into the river and says—"

"I know what he says," Gigi interrupted. "One line. Big deal."

"It's not just one line. George wants—"

"George *thinks* he wants more than what he has. But in the end he realizes that his life is a great deal more meaningful than he thought."

"I went to film school, Gigi. Did a whole term on Capra."

"Apparently you need to repeat the course, hon."

4

May

ON A CLEAR spring day, Lou finally braced herself and told her mother she'd quit the job Estelle herself had worked so hard to land for her—by endlessly singing Lou's praises to her mah-jongg partner, Harvey's mother Bunny. A follow-up phone call from her father had been inevitable. He'd undoubtedly been pushed to do the deed by Estelle, who knew she'd be in big trouble if she were to call again.

"Sweetheart! What's doin'?"

"You know darn well what's doing, Dad. What's doing with you? How's your arthritis? Mom says it's been acting up."

"Oh, you know. Listen, you get to my age and if it's not one thing, it's another—arthritis, gallstones, the prostate, God forbid—"

"Right. Well, you're doing pretty well, Dad, considering."

"Hey, watch it! What are you trying to do? Jinx me?"

"Wouldn't dream of it. Sorry."

"Honey—" Freddy's voice grew concerned "—what's this I hear about your quitting your job?"

Lou sighed. Freddy was a lot more easygoing than Estelle—who wasn't?—but a conversation with him could be equally draining due to his utter and total confusion about modern life. "Dad, don't worry," she said, aiming for an unconcerned tone, even though she'd awakened in a panic that morning, drenched with sweat. *You have a nest egg,* she'd repeated to herself for about the millionth time since quitting Harvey Gold. "It's not like when you worked for Snappy Garments. People don't toil for the same companies all their lives anymore. They flit from job to job. It's the normal thing."

"Never mind that. I worry, I worry," Fred said. "So does your mother. And as for that high-falutin' ex-boyfriend of yours—"

She *had* told her parents about Alan soon after the breakup. Clearly they still hadn't gotten over it. "Dad, I already told you, it was mutual," Lou lied. She couldn't let Estelle and Freddy know the truth about Alan after all those years of defending him. One could *never* let parents know that they'd actually been right about a boyfriend.

"So are you going to stay in the apartment? Can you afford it? Do you have another job lined—"

"Dad, stop! Everything will be fine. I have a couple of projects on the go and if it gets to the point where I can't afford the apartment any longer, I'll get a roommate or move."

"What?" Freddy was listening to a series of loud commands in the background. "Your mother says be careful with a roommate. Kitty Sherman's niece was assaulted by a potential roommate—"

"Lou?" Estelle had grabbed the phone. "Listen to me. Do not advertise for a roommate. Find one through a friend you can trust. Kitty Sherman's niece—"

"Yes, I know, Mom," Lou said tiredly. "Dad just told me."

"Just so you know," Estelle said, a little deflated. She perked up. "Speaking of Kitty, I just saw her son Michael—"

"Mom, I'm on my way out. I have a date." Okay, not exactly true, but she wasn't up to having this conversation with her parents.

"A date!" Estelle called to Fred, "She has a date!" She got back on the phone. "So, who is he?"

"Oh...nobody you know."

"What does he do?"

"He—owns a coffee chain." Lou sent a silent apology to Jake for conveniently using him.

"A chain! Very nice. Well, don't let me hold you up. Have a nice time."

"I will." Suddenly, Lou felt bad about cutting Estelle off. "Look, Mom, I'll call you later, okay?"

"We'll be asleep later. Call me tomorrow. Let me know how your date went."

"Okay, Ma."

She hung up and thought for a moment.

Maybe a date with Jake wasn't such a bad idea. An evening with him would surely take her mind off the fact that her life wasn't changing nearly quickly enough for her liking. Her writing had stalled and, although her nest egg was still fairly hefty, it was beginning to dwindle. She definitely needed a distraction, so why *not* take Jake up on the challenge he'd presented after their evening at the Sacred Squash and prove that *his* lifestyle was the ridiculous one?

She could barely believe it was really her, standing in the doorway of his loft—the address of which she'd commandeered from a surprised Pauline—just an hour later, saying, "Get dressed, mister. We're going to dinner."

She had made reservations at Steakfrites, a hot new midtown steakhouse. It was worth blowing a portion of her nest egg, she thought, on proving a rich guy wrong.

Jake, looking fabulous, as usual—a Gucci ad today in a white open-collared shirt and flat-front black pants—let out a long, low whistle after looking her up and down. Lou tried not to let on that she was pleased. She'd spent about three hours getting ready, even though she was wearing just a very simple black leather skirt with a close-fitting white T-shirt and low-heeled black sling-backs.

"You look good enough to devour," he said, leering. "What say we stay here?"

"Not a chance." She sauntered in. "We're going to Steakfrites."

"Steakfrites." He lifted a brow as he closed the door. "Wow. How did you get a reservation?"

"An old film school friend is the hostess."

He shook his head. "See what happens when you don't sell out?"

While he excused himself to freshen up, Lou took the liberty of checking out his loft living room. Jake lived in a new building in the same area as she did, but it might as well have been a different world. This apartment was luxury Alan could only have dreamed of. She had to admit, the place was fabulous, complete with a brand-new kitchen outfitted with restaurant-quality appliances, a series of complicated lighting systems, imported furnishings—she could just tell—and original art on the walls.

When he emerged from his bedroom, he caught Lou studying his CD collection.

"Great collection," she commented. "I didn't know you like jazz."

"Oh, yeah. I'm into everything—Coltrane, Bennett, you name it."

"I'm impressed."

He grinned devilishly. "I live to impress."

She made a face at him. "Ready?"

"You bet. We're walking, I presume."

"It's only a few blocks. Unless you can't take it."

"Outta here, Bergman, let's go."

They walked to Steakfrites, just ten blocks north on 59th Street and Lou didn't miss the many glances shot in Jake's direction from female passersby, which irked her immensely until she realized she was getting her fair share from the male passersby. Jake seemed immune to it all, happily humming as they walked in virtual lockstep toward the restaurant.

"Shame to stop to eat," Jake commented. "We have such a good rhythm going."

Lou rolled her eyes. "That makes no sense. It's like the parking thing."

Jake grinned. "It's just as hard to find a walker with a matching stride as it is to find a good parking spot. It's not a thing to be taken lightly."

As he opened the door of Steakfrites, he looked deeply into her eyes. Her heart skipped a few beats.

"*Après vous, mademoiselle,*" he murmured.

"You need a new line," she said, hoping he couldn't hear her heart hammering away. Once it had started working again, it had *really* started working.

It took about ten minutes to even get to the hostess once they had stepped through the door.

"Tracy, over here!" Lou practically shouted to get her friend's attention away from the crowd clamoring for her attention.

Tracy made her way over to Lou and Jake and said loudly, "Follow me. I've got a table for you. It's crazy here tonight."

She led them through the restaurant to a table that Lou thought she wouldn't want to move a thing on, let alone disturb with plates of food.

"Wow," was all she said.

Tracy nodded. "Wow is right. No expense was spared."

"Joel Silver does everything first-class," Jake commented.

"Exactly." Tracy extended her hand. "I'm Tracy, an old friend of Lou's."

"Oh, sorry, Trace," Lou said. "This is Jake Roth. Jake, Tracy."

"Charmed," he said.

"Likewise," she said, looking at him admiringly. She pulled out a chair first for Lou—with Lou protesting and Trace saying, "It's my job, girl!"—then for Jake. "Well, enjoy, you two. I'd better get back to the madding crowd."

"I take it you know the owner, then?" Lou asked.

He shrugged. "We're acquainted." He looked around. "Nice, huh?"

Lou followed his glance. Nice wasn't the word. It was awesome—filled with the same kind of impressive furnishings and artwork as Jake's apartment. She shrugged. "It's okay."

He looked amused. "Okay?"

Just then the sommelier appeared at the table. "Have you had a chance to look at the wine list?" She was gorgeous and turned a brilliant smile on Jake.

Lou was mentally formulating a speech about how the staff in places like these discriminated against women, when the sommelier turned an equally brilliant smile on her.

Jake started to speak, but Lou interrupted. She had invited Jake, after all, and she knew what she could and couldn't afford. "The house red, please. A bottle."

Surprisingly, the sommelier smiled and nodded, without batting an eyelash. After she left, Jake said, "I'm not going to let you pay for this, Lou."

"Of course you are. I asked you here, remember?"

"Only because I asked you first."

"You didn't ask me, you challenged me."

"I never thought you'd take up the challenge."

"You underestimated me."

"Apparently I did." He looked at her intently and she felt flustered momentarily. Luckily, she was saved by the arrival of a waiter.

Jake gave a dazzling smile to the server. "Good evening, sir."

"Good evening to you, and to you, ma'am." He smiled pleasantly and handed them menus. "The specials are listed on the insert. I'll be back in a few minutes to take your orders."

"Thank you," Jake said.

When the waiter was gone, he commented, "Nice server. Not too pushy or palsy-walsy." He paused. "Or neurotic."

Lou glared, knowing he was referring to their waitress at the Sacred Squash. "I think it's a little too early in the game to judge," she said. But somehow she knew the service would be perfect. She turned her attention to the menu. "Wow. I'm bowled over. Steak, steak or steak." In truth, her mouth was watering in anticipation. She hadn't eaten a good steak in ages.

"What are you talking about? There's plenty of variety. There's even steak tartare—raw steak. That capital-I Interesting enough for you?"

"Jake, this menu is stuck in the 1950s."

"There's a retro nod. But it's not as if the Sacred Squash oozed originality."

Lou couldn't help but smile. "Point taken."

He smiled back.

"What are you smiling about?" she asked suspiciously.

"That poetry—"

"Spoken word art, if you please."

They both laughed.

Just then a handsome man in a suit who was going from table to table came over to theirs, extended a hand toward Jake and said, "Great to see you, buddy. Enjoying yourself, I hope?"

Jake shook the other man's hand warmly. "A-1 so far, Joel, thanks. Joel, this is Lou Bergman. Lou, Joel Silver, co-owner of this fine establishment."

"Lou, a pleasure." Joel extended his hand and Lou shook it, feeling like a princess. He turned back to Jake. "So, will I see you at that Desmond and Burns thing next week?" The men began an animated conversation about the merits of one sort of investment over another and Lou politely excused herself to go to the washroom.

When she came back, Joel exited smoothly and Lou said to Jake, "So how do you two know each other? Meetings of the Rich Restaurateurs Club?"

Jake grinned. "Nothing so glamorous. We play floor hockey together. And I usually see him at the barber's."

Just then, their wine arrived. The sommelier poured the wine for Jake, who tasted it and approved.

After she poured Lou a glass, she smiled, said, "Enjoy," and left gracefully.

"Is it really okay?" Lou asked Jake as he took another tentative sip.

"It's okay for cheap crap. But sometimes I enjoy drinking cheap crap."

"Stick with me, kid."

He smiled. "Mean it?" He didn't wait for her to respond. "Wait a second—we didn't even make a toast!"

Lou lifted her glass obligingly. "What should we toast to?"

"To learning about how the other half lives."

"I'll drink to that," she said, thinking that, even though

she generally hated these kinds of places, she was really having a terrific time.

When she heard Gigi's voice say, *Told you so*, she gagged.

"Are you all right?" Jake asked, concerned.

"F-fine," she sputtered. She'd never get used to this. Wasn't it only crazy people who heard voices?

Lou, I can't tell you the good it does me to see you listen to your heart, finally!

"I'm not listening to my heart!" Lou cried.

"Your heart? What's the matter with your heart?" Jake said, alarmed.

"Nothing, nothing," Lou assured him

"You want to leave? You're not feeling well?"

Lou sighed. "No. I'm sorry, Jake." She studied the menu without seeing it.

Lou, listen to your heart. You're having such a good time here!

That's enough! I want more out of life than fancy restaurants and a swanky apartment!

What makes you think Jake is unable to give you more?

Is there anything wrong with taking a breather—taking some time to decide what I want to do rather than just drift into some relationship because it's there for the taking? I took the job at Harvey Gold because it was safe. I've had it with playing it safe.

There's nothing intrinsically wrong with security, Lou.

But you can't blame me for experimenting—career- or relationship-wise—can you? I've never done it.

Jake cleared his throat and said, "Lou, are you okay?"

She looked up from her menu and smiled brilliantly. "Perfect. Couldn't be better. Where were we?"

He looked at her carefully. "We were making a toast." He lifted his glass back up. She followed suit. "To learning how the other half lives...and to friendship," he said.

Just then, their waiter returned. "Have you decided?"

"Oh," Lou said, glancing quickly at her menu, "I'll have the Caesar salad and the filet mignon, medium-rare, please."

"Same for me," Jake said.

"Good choice," the server said. "It shouldn't take too long."

When he left, Jake leaned back in his chair. "So, tell me about what you've been doing lately."

She lifted a brow. "You really want to know?"

"I really want to know."

"Well, I've been working on my screenplay," she said, omitting the part about having been unable to write a word for the past two weeks, six days, nine hours and twenty-five minutes. *Two weeks is nothing,* she told herself for the umpteenth time.

Unless it stretches into two months or two years, she heard Gigi say.

"Good for you," Jake said.

"Oh, so you approve?"

"I'm in your corner, Lou."

"Could have fooled me," she muttered. What was the whole bet thing if not a determined effort to prove she was going about her life all wrong?

"Are you doing anything part-time to bring in some steady money?"

She glared at him. "Now you sound like my father."

He held up a hand. "Heaven forbid."

She sighed. "I do have a nest egg, you know. I wouldn't have quit my job if I didn't. But I don't want to completely deplete it. I'm thinking about starting up a film zine that, hopefully, will bring in some extra cash." The thought had occurred to her just moments earlier, after Gigi had made her crack about the writer's block possibly lasting forever. Lou had spent a few seconds racking her brain for ideas and had come up with the zine plan, which she thought was brilliant. No one could accuse a zine publisher of selling out and it definitely beat working in a coffee shop.

"A magazine. Great! I should introduce you to—"

"A zine, not a magazine."

He looked puzzled. "Correct me if I'm wrong, but isn't 'zine' short for 'magazine'?"

"Not in this context. A zine is a homemade magazine—done with computers and photocopiers."

"Ah, capital-I Interesting people making magazines."

"Right."

"Sounds like a plan." After a moment he said, "So you really hated the wedding business, huh?"

"I don't know if I hated it," she said slowly. "Even though I razz Nic about the biz, it's not all that bad. It just wasn't me."

"What part wasn't you? I'm not criticizing," he said quickly. "I'm just curious."

She shrugged. "I dunno. Harvey specializes in Long Island circus weddings."

"I like those weddings. They're fun."

Lou cocked a brow. "You don't strike me as the Long Island type."

"Who knows? When I have a family, I'd consider moving out there. Wouldn't want my kids to become overprivileged-Manhattan-private-school types."

Lou was surprised and was about to tell him so when their salads arrived. She ate a forkful. It was heavenly. The lettuce tasted as if it had just been plucked from the fields. The garlicky croutons were enormous and sensational. And there were generous shavings of a delicious Parmigianno-Reggiano throughout. When their main courses arrived, they both tried the filet mignon at the same time.

Lou nearly groaned with pleasure. It was buttery-soft and full of delicate flavorings.

Jake grinned. "Not bad, huh?"

"Not bad," Lou said casually.

Jake shook his head. "You're a stubborn woman, Lou Bergman."

"That I am, Jake Roth."

"SO, I SHOULD COME UP so we can critique the meal some more," Jake said when they stopped at the corner of her building.

"Not a chance," Lou said firmly.

"Afraid you'll admit it was good?" he teased.

"Never."

He moved a bit closer to her. "So what, exactly, are you afraid of?"

She moved away. "What makes you think I'm afraid of something?" she said as nonchalantly as she could, hoping he couldn't hear her heart slam against her chest.

"We're just friends, right?"

"Friends. Yup. That's right."

"So," he said in a wheedling tone, "friends can have a nightcap together, watch some TV, listen to music. It's still pretty early."

Lou glanced at her watch. It *was* still early. But there was no way she would ever let Jake Roth set foot in her apartment. She couldn't trust herself to be alone with him.

"Speak for yourself," she said, thinking as fast as she could. "You think these great looks come naturally? I have to get my beauty sleep."

He looked at her. "You are great-looking, you know."

Her heart skipped a beat, but she just rolled her eyes. "Right." She looked at him. "Not next to all those model types at Steakfrites. Which is another reason I don't like restaurants like the one we went to tonight—they make you feel so bad about yourself. Every woman in there looked as if she'd just come back from a spa vacation."

"Every woman in there probably did just come back from a spa vacation," Jake said dryly.

"Exactly!" Lou was warming up to her topic now. "Don't you think there's something wrong with that constant attention to appearances—surfaces? You don't feel you can even set foot in a place like that unless you're at your very best, looks-wise."

He leaned toward her and moved her chin so that she was looking into his eyes.

She gulped.

"Lou, you were the most beautiful woman in that place tonight."

She laughed nervously. "Sure. Next thing you'll be telling me I could win a beauty contest."

"You could," he murmured, leaning closer.

She was afraid to breathe.

She closed her eyes when he placed his lips softly on hers.

Sweet agony...she thought as she kissed him back.

She pulled away breathlessly and began to walk backward to the front door. "So, thanks for a great dinner."

She couldn't see his face in the shadows, which was probably a good thing, she told herself as she turned on her heel and ran inside. If she had seen even a trace of leftover desire in his eyes, she would have been a goner.

5

June

Lou sighed before opening the door to the Havajava. She'd reluctantly agreed to meet Nic's and Pauline's new doctor beaus. The two had lucked out at a hospital fundraiser, which Lou hadn't attended because she could no longer afford to spread her funds around.

Great, Lou thought dismally. Her pals would be snuggling up with their doctors while she hugged her...bowl of decaf latte. Why the heck had she agreed to the rendezvous?

Because you don't have so many friends that you can afford to lose these two, she thought glumly as she entered.

"Lou," Nic screeched, waving excitedly, "over here!"

Lou pasted on a smile and headed over to the table.

"Hey, Lou," Pauline said, shooting her a smile back and a look that seemed to indicate she sympathized. If Lou had had a date herself, that would have been one thing, but now she was doomed to act the part of the sidekick, the amusing and eccentric single pal of those most likely to pair off and breed.

"Hey yourself," Lou said.

"Lou," Nic piped up, "this—" she put her arm around her genial-looking paediatric surgeon date and he beamed "—is Peter Hamlin." He was wearing a T-shirt with a

teddy bear on it, Lou noted. He seemed perfect for Nic.
"Peter, my great friend, Lou."

"Good to meet you, Lou," Peter said genially.

"Same here," Lou said, aiming for an equal level of ge-
niality and failing.

"Lou, this is Rob Lewis ," Pauline said.

"Good to meet you, Lou," Rob said, extending a hand.
His tone and demeanor told Lou instantly that this was a
person of high intelligence, though she got the feeling he
wasn't incapable of irreverence.

"Nice to meet you, too," Lou said. "Let me just go to the
counter for my coffee. We'll chat when I get back."

She was grateful for the small reprieve.

Zooey, the multipierced dropout who worked evenings
and weekends, was at the counter. Her hair was green.

"Hey," Lou said, "how's my favorite rock star?" Lou
had learned some time ago that Zooey had a rock band
called Zooey's Animals. They rehearsed during the day
and played gigs that began when their various night shifts
ended.

Zooey snapped her gum and sighed. "Life pretty much
sucks this week. My drummer's depressed 'cuz his ferret
died and my keyboardist is in rehab."

"Bummer," Lou said.

"The usual?" Zooey asked.

"Please."

As Zooey got her coffee, Lou said, "So, what happens to
your gigs? Do you have to cancel?"

Zooey sighed, handed Lou her coffee and said, "Yeah.
We were booked at two new places this week. They'll
never ask us back once I pull out." She rung up Lou's order.

"So don't pull out. Why don't you perform solo?" She
handed Zooey her money.

Zooey snapped her gum again. "I never thought of that. I've only ever played in bands. But I guess, yeah, I'd do it—just me and my guitar." She smiled. "Taz can be my roadie."

"Taz?"

"My boyfriend."

"You have a boyfriend?" Lou smiled. "That's nice."

"Yeah. Taz is great. He's really normal."

"Normal?" Lou wondered what Zooey's definition of normal was.

She got her answer shortly. "Yeah, not a screwed-up musician."

"What does he do?"

"IT."

"IT?"

"Yeah, you know—information technology? He works for IBM."

Lou pondered this a moment, wondering if she'd just stepped into an alternate universe. "Your boyfriend works for IBM?"

"Yeah." Zooey smiled dreamily. "He wants to buy me a house in the 'burbs."

Lou let this second shocker sink in. "He doesn't sound much like the roadie type," she said after a moment.

Zooey grinned. "You'd be surprised. He helps us out a lot. But lately he's been really busy at work and he's zonked at night, so yeah, you're right, that probably wouldn't work. Maybe I'll just quit the music business."

"Zooey, no—you can't! It's your passion—your life!"

"She wants to quit, let her quit," Lauren the Rich Girl said from behind Lou.

"What's *your* passion, Lauren—shopping?" added Ingrid snidely from a nearby table.

Zooey rolled her eyes. "It isn't my life. It was fun for a

while, but it's kind of, well, kid stuff. Maybe it's time I grew up."

"What're we talking about?" Zee, the biker, asked. He'd just come in and was standing behind Lauren.

"Zooey wants to give her music thing up, Lou says she can't, but Zooey says it's not her dream," Dent, the trucker, said from a table where he was sitting with Sam, the nerdy depressive.

"If she says it's not, it's not," Zee said to Lou. "You have to be passionate about your dream. If you're not passionate about it, it's not the right dream."

"So says the man passionate about delivering envelopes to wealthy corporations on a bike," Lauren said sarcastically.

Zee glared at her.

"But she's so young—how can she know what she really wants?" Lou pleaded.

"Give it up, Lou," Sam said. "Even if it is her dream, it's not worth it if she can't make ends meet."

"I thought you've been miserable since giving up your dream?" Ingrid demanded.

"I have been," Sam said mournfully, "but I was miserable trying to make my pen protector business work, too."

"Maybe you didn't stick it out long enough," said Dent.

"I stuck it out for years!" Sam said angrily. "Just because your thing worked and mine didn't—"

"Hey, easy, guys," Zee said, holding up a hand.

"Dreams are funny things," Ingrid mused.

"Yeah, but you heard Zooey," Ted, sitting with Ingrid, said. "She's growing up. She's dreaming new dreams."

Lou struggled valiantly to form the right words. "But growing up doesn't have to mean conforming to society's expectations and giving up—"

"Who's giving up?" Zooey said, exasperated. "The

band was just something to do, you know?" She snapped her gum and smiled again. "I'm thinking it would be nice to have a little cottage in the suburbs, with a picket fence around it...."

"Nobody makes picket fences anymore," Lou told her. "Only pressure-treated wood ones that leach dangerous levels of arsenic into the soil—"

"That's a myth," Lauren said enthusiastically. "My daddy's in lumber and he said so."

Zooey looked at Lou. "Lou, there are customers behind you."

Lou grunted and headed to her table. When she got back, Peter said heartily, "So, Lou, I've heard so much about you."

Lou sighed inwardly. No doubt Nic had told him all about her best friend's pathetically troubled life. Peter had probably received strict instructions to talk Lou's ear off, seeing as she was all alone, poor baby....

"Nic tells me you're working on a screenplay. That's so exciting. How's it going?"

"Yeah, how's it going, Lou? I'm dying to know." That was Jake, pulling up a chair beside her. He shot her an admiring gaze, even though tonight she was just wearing faded old jeans and a white T-shirt. He matched, a Marlboro Man tonight, in faded jeans, a white T-shirt and cowboy boots. "Hey, Rob, how are you doing? And you must be Peter." He extended a hand to Nic's beau. "Jake Roth. I'm Pauline's cousin and the owner of this fine establishment." He turned back to Lou and pierced her with that laser-blue gaze. "So, how *is* it going, Lou?"

"Great. Everything's peachy," she said glumly. Her screenplay was still stalled and her zine was taking shape at a snail's pace.

He grinned. She had to ask.

"Do you bleach your teeth?"

"Um—no."

Lou turned back to the doctors, who were looking a little puzzled. She hadn't missed the look Rob had given Pauline that seemed to say, "*This* is your best friend?" or the one Pauline had shot back indicating that he should have patience. She decided to bring them back into the conversation.

"So, Rob, is the ER really like *E.R.*?"

He smiled, relieved. Clearly, once upon a time, she had learned manners somewhere. "Nope, not by a long shot. We're the ugliest bunch you've ever seen."

"Hey, what about us pediatric guys?" Peter said in an aggrieved tone. "Those fake noses and elephant-covered hats really do a number on our naturally rugged good looks."

All laughed and the tension was mercifully broken. They seemed like good guys, which Lou was grateful for since for the next few decades, they'd be forced to live with her constant presence in their homes.

"This is a great place, Jake," Peter commented.

"Glad you like it. We're expanding and there's going to be one right beside the hospital. Can I count on your business?"

"You've got mine," Rob said. "This coffee is fabulous."

"Rob's somewhat of a gourmet," Pauline explained.

"That right, Rob?" Peter said. "Best I can do is chicken pot pie, I'm afraid." He smiled at Nic, who snuggled up to him and held on to his arm tightly. "I'm the son of a country doctor. Mom did all the cooking, I'm ashamed to say."

"Not to worry, hon, I'm a great cook," Nic said, squeezing his arm.

"Rob made me this fabulous sea bass last night," Pauline said, smiling at her man.

Can I throw up now? Lou thought.

"No kidding?" Nic said. "How do you make that, Rob?"

"I wrap it in parchment paper with a fresh salsa made with tomatoes cilantro, and..."

Lou tuned out and turned away.

Jake watched her.

"Would you excuse us for a minute, ladies and gentlemen?" he said suddenly, grabbing Lou's elbow. "I have something I want to show Lou."

"You do?" she said as he pulled her up.

"Yes, remember? The thing upstairs?"

"Oh, yes, the thing upstairs back. Right. We'll be back in a flash, everybody."

"So, what did you want to show me?" she asked once they were in Jake's office. Damn, she thought. Even she could hear the nervousness in her voice.

"My etchings," Jake said, grinning and waggling his eyebrows.

"Seriously."

"Seriously, my etchings. Here, take a look."

He withdrew sketches of Pauline and Nic from a file drawer in his desk and laid them out on the desktop.

"I did one of each in charcoal and the other set in pastel. Which do you prefer?"

Lou whistled. "They're all terrific. You did these?"

"Guilty as charged."

"Wow, where did you learn—"

"I've been drawing as long as I can remember."

"Did you have some kind of formal training?"

"Nah, I just fool around."

Lou studied the drawings. "I don't know anything about art, but I know talent when I see it. You could definitely sell your stuff."

He shrugged. "Maybe." Then he smiled. "I have one for

you, too." From the drawer he pulled out a sketch with her looking like Audrey Hepburn in *Breakfast at Tiffany's*. She was looking up at the sky thoughtfully and all around the margin were scribbled the words "Where to live? What to do? Who to date?"

"It's beautiful," she said after a moment.

He studied her. "Yeah, I think I came pretty close to getting you."

She looked back. "So you don't think you...got me?"

"I don't think anyone will ever really get you, Lou," he said.

"Aha, so you admit I'm not just some typical upper West Sider," she said, trying to keep things light.

"Not even close," he murmured.

There was an awkward moment of silence and then Lou said something she probably shouldn't have. Of course, she didn't realize that until immediately after she said it.

"Don't you ever feel bad about—I don't know—not using your talent to its full capacity?"

He looked at her carefully. "And by that you mean not working full time at art?"

She started to object, but he said, "I'm always making art. The only thing I'm not doing is making my living from it. That's what you object to, right? My being a business owner?"

"Yes—no, of course not! I don't know. You're confusing me," Lou said.

"Am I?" Jake answered. "Sorry. Don't mean to."

She looked at him. "Don't you?"

He stared back.

They were silent for a moment.

"I have a question for you," Lou said finally.

"What?"

"Apparently you're happy where you are but I'm not

happy where I am. Why are you so against my...journey? Sorry, I hate that word."

"I'm not against your journey. Hell, that bet was a bit of a joke, Lou. I wouldn't dream of telling you what to do. But I do have some experience in this area. I had to go all around the world to figure out that I still wanted to live on the West Side of Manhattan, and that I could be a business owner if I wanted to, 'Interesting' society's judgment be damned."

"Where did you go?" Lou asked curiously.

"Oh, you know, the usual lost graduate tour—Thailand, India, parts of Europe, parts of Africa. Worked everywhere I went. Helped set up community projects, taught English."

"Really? Wow."

He looked at her. "I didn't want to be like my parents."

"So, what made you—"

He shrugged. "After a while, I realized I wanted to make my home here. I love New York. And I kept getting ideas for businesses. I've always had a head for it. I was tired of fighting it. So I decided to set something up and do art as a hobby."

She almost said something, then hesitated.

"What?" Jake demanded.

She took a breath. "Could it be that you're afraid of finding out what the pros think of your artwork?"

Jake pinned a gaze on her that stopped just short of steely.

"I'm sorry, Jake. I didn't mean—"

"Didn't you?" He strode over to the door and held it open for her, saying, "The bet's still on, Lou."

6

IT WAS IRONIC how, ever since telling Lou art was strictly a hobby, Jake had been feeling the urge to paint more and more. As he half-heartedly studied a supplier invoice one morning, he reminded himself that there was no way he could ever make a comfortable living as an artist in New York City. He also reminded himself of how his parents had constantly praised his business acumen. Clearly he'd made the right decision going to business school over art school. He could still paint and draw in his spare time. That was what hobbies were for, right?

He was happy. Perfectly happy.

Wasn't he?

WHILE HANGING OUT at the Havajava with the girls, Lou announced her intention to run a classified advertisement for a capital-I Interesting boyfriend. Jake had been right. It *was* his livelihood that was stopping her from getting involved with him. The last thing she wanted was another materialist-conformist in her life—even one who sketched occasionally. But even Bohemians had men in their lives. She missed having a significant other—missed the "everydayness" of it, the companionship.

Not to mention the sex.

"It's a bad idea, Lou," Pauline warned her. Nic echoed the sentiment.

As per their predictions, most of the responses Lou received two weeks later just couldn't be taken seriously.

"Although," Lou told Pauline at her apartment—they were sitting cross-legged on the floor, close to a giant bowl of Orville Redenbacher's popcorn— "having opted for the newspaper over the Internet, I cut the number of respondents, and therefore the number of psychotic respondents, approximately in half."

"I'm not sure about that," Pauline said. "Listen to this. 'Massage therapist promises soulful love and all the free massages you desire in exchange for room and board in a decent building, decent meaning no rats, roaches or crack dealers within a two-block radius.'"

"I don't give guarantees,". Lou said.

"You sure?" Pauline asked. "Soulful love and free massages sound pretty good to me."

"Why don't *you* answer, then?"

"He'd probably sue me for invasion of privacy or something. Studies have shown that even the most centered and balanced New Yorker is approximately three hundred percent more litigious than the average inhabitant of any other major urban city."

"I'm hoping you made that up," Lou said.

"I did," Pauline confessed.

"Well," Lou said, holding up another letter, "if the massage therapist doesn't appeal to you, there's always the Russian whose mail-order bride was a big disappointment. Get a load of this. 'I am Russian man. My mail-order bride was man dressed to be girl. I come see instead you. We to have good sex. My thing very big to make scream the women. You give me money and to live in nice American place. Is a deal?'"

"That has to be a joke," Pauline said, snatching the paper. "Jeez, he signed his name in Russian. It's real." She shook her head, tossed the Russian's letter into the Ignore pile and picked up another one. She whistled after a few seconds. "Another winner. Listen to this. 'Having been abducted by aliens no less than twenty times in two months, I can promise you the trip of a lifetime. If you're looking for a capital-I Interesting life, as you said in your ad, this is it! Last time, my abductors said they wanted me to have a female partner for the next session. We'll have to live together right off the bat because I never know when they're going to come back. Warning—the probes are quite painful, but it's worth it.'"

"Way to sell a lifestyle, Spaceman," Lou said, still trying to remain chipper as she skimmed the responses, though extreme discouragement was setting in. What had ever possessed her to do this? What were the chances she'd meet her soul mate through an *advertisement*? But wait a minute.... What was this?

"Okay, now we're getting somewhere," she said excitedly. "This one's a definite possibility."

"It's a trick," Pauline said flatly.

"No, listen. 'Hi, Lou. My name is Jim James. I'm a not-so-bad-looking musician—slim, blond hair, blue eyes—who's probably slightly more Interesting than the greedy jerks you've been hanging out with. You sound pretty cool and I'd like to meet you. I like strong coffee and jazz music. Hope you do, too. Talk to you later? Jim.'"

Pauline swallowed a piece of popcorn and said, "Lou, I really think you should just chalk this whole thing up to experience. We had some laughs and some really good popcorn. There has to be something wrong with this guy. His psychosis is just well hidden."

"I want to meet him."

Pauline rolled her eyes. "What if he's a vicious lunatic?"

"I'll meet him at Starbucks." She didn't want to have to explain the rendezvous to any of her Havajava friends. Especially the Havajava's owner. "You can plant yourself there. When it comes time to leave, I'll 'bump into' you and we'll leave together. Nothing can happen while we're there."

Pauline sighed. "I don't know…"

Lou held up the photograph Jim had sent. "You're asking me to give up this possibility?"

Pauline looked at Lou. "Are you doing this because you're mad at Jake?"

"I'm not mad at Jake. He's mad at me." She paused. "Pauline, Jake and I would never work—"

Pauline held up a hand. "None of my business. I don't want to get in the middle of it. I just don't want you two to be enemies."

"We're not enemies." Lou looked out a window. "It's this stupid bet thing. Your cousin seems to thrive on conflict." It was close enough to the truth, she thought.

"He must get that from his father's side. Our mothers were sisters," Pauline added.

"Ah, so that explains your lack of millions. The other sister married better."

Pauline laughed. "My mom did pretty well, too." She eyed Lou. "You think once this bet thing is over, you two will be able to go back to normal?"

Lou shifted on the floor. "Yeah, sure. Why not?"

Pauline frowned. "I don't believe you."

Lou lifted the Jim James photograph. "Meeting Jim will put me in a much better frame of mind."

Pauline sighed. "Okay, I give, I give."

"Maybe we should meet at a café downtown," Lou mused out loud. "He is a musician, after all…"

"Forget it—it's Starbucks or bust," Pauline said.

Lou chose Starbucks, but wished she'd chosen bust one week later, when a person who looked nothing like Jim's picture sidled up to her holding a coffee and said, "Lou?"

"Uh, yes?"

"Jim!"

"You're Jim? But—" *But you're definitely not slim, and you have greasy, uncombed brown hair, not to mention eerily vacant-looking brown eyes.*

"But I look nothing like my picture." He smirked. "I know. It's my cousin Ben. If I'd sent you my picture, would you have set up this date?"

Lou avoided answering him, just smiled and gestured to the chair opposite her. "Have a seat."

As he heaved himself into the chair, she saw Pauline roll her eyes and heard Gigi's sigh in her head.

Jim was smiling—a smile that made her extremely uneasy.

"So, you're a musician," she said, determined to remain calm. "How did you get into music?"

He waved a hand. "Oh, God, I've been making music since I was in diapers."

"Really? Wow. And now you've made your childhood dream come true. What instruments do you play? Have you recorded anything?"

"I, uh, play just about everything, and I dabble in a variety of styles," he said vaguely.

"Rock, jazz, country...?"

"Oh, I've done it all."

Lou was suspicious now. "What do you do the most of?"

"Oh—you know. Whatever my fans like."

"Whatever your fans like."

Jim shifted in his chair.

"Are you a soloist? Part of a band? A studio musician? Songwriter?"

Jim looked surprised at that question and, after a moment, said, "I fly solo now, but sure, I've been in bands and done the studio thing."

"What was the name of your band?"

"Caffeine," he said triumphantly.

Lou crossed her arms. "Who did you do studio work for?"

Jim didn't have a studio work answer on the tip of his tongue. He stuttered and stammered until Lou finally stood and said, "Jim—if that's really your name—I don't think you're being honest with me and I don't want to waste my time with a liar. So I'm going to say goodbye now."

"All men are liars," he called as she left, grabbing Pauline along the way. "You're living in fantasyland!"

They didn't stop until they were inside the Havajava. Once they were sitting, Lou covered her head in her hands. "Please don't say I told you so."

"I never say I told you so."

Lou sighed. "What a waste of a Tracey Faith dress." She looked down at the yellow gingham halter dress—very retro chic—and sighed again. "I really am living in fantasyland, aren't I?"

"It can be a pretty nice place," Pauline said.

"So you think it's true?"

Pauline shrugged. "Your standards are pretty high. But it's hard to know where to draw the line. Except with total idiots like Jim. With other, decent guys, sometimes it's hard to know whether you're settling or just being realistic."

"How do you feel about Rob?"

After a moment Pauline said thoughtfully, "It's early

days, but I don't think I would ever feel like I was settling with Rob."

Lou threw her hands in the air. "See, there you go. I've *never* felt that. I've never been absolutely sure about anyone."

"I didn't say I was absolutely sure about him," Pauline corrected her. "Lord knows he has his flaws—as I have mine—and I've wondered about whether I can handle some of them."

"Well, I've never even been that close," Lou said, darting a lethal glance at a young couple making out at the next table. "I thought it was because I was dating boring, materialistic guys, but the interesting ones are turning out to be even screwier." She stood. "C'mon, let's get our coffees."

At the counter, a purple-haired Zooey looked at Lou and said, "Bad day?"

"Bad month," Pauline said for her. "Bad year."

Zooey sighed. "Me, too. Taz got offered a vice presidency, but he'll have to move out of state to the head office."

Lou stared. "Taz is going to be a vice president at IBM?"

"Maybe," Zooey said. "Your usuals?"

"Yup," Lou said, still in shock. After a moment she said, "That's sad...that Taz has to move."

"Oh, I might go with him."

"Has he...asked you to go with him?" Lou asked carefully, suddenly certain that the would-be IBM V.P. was married.

"Oh, yeah," Zooey said cheerfully. "Practically begged me. Got right down on his hands and knees." She snapped her gum and giggled. "He said Christmas parties wouldn't be any fun without me to liven them up." She handed them their coffees and sobered. "But I'll definitely have to give up my band."

"What happened with those gigs a couple weeks back? Did you cancel or go solo?"

Zooey perked up. "I did them solo. They went great. Thanks for the idea."

"You're welcome," Lou said. "So if you're solo now, what's the problem? You can work anywhere."

"Oh, I just did those gigs solo so the club owners wouldn't be pissed. The band is still together."

"Ah. So the depressed drummer and the drug addict are doing well?"

"Not really," Zooey confessed.

"Oh," Lou said. She didn't quite know what to say to that, so she just handed Zooey a bill. "For me and Pauline," she said.

"Thanks," Pauline said. "Good luck with your decision," she said to Zooey.

Zooey nodded.

Back at the table Lou muttered, "I get Jim James, she gets Taz the part-time groupie who also happens to be an IBM V.P."

"But you don't want an IBM V.P.," Pauline reminded her. "You want a capital-I Interesting person. A full time groupie, maybe?"

"Ha, ha," Lou said grumpily.

Just then they saw Nic come in and dazzle the fused pair at the next table with a brilliant, approving smile. She saw Pauline and Lou, waved excitedly and made her way over to their table.

"I can't believe I ran into you guys!" She followed Lou's eyes to the canoodling couple at the next table, then turned back to her friend. "They're gonna melt if you keep looking at them like that," she said. "Ease up, would ya?"

"Well, look who's here," Pauline said, pulling a chair over from an empty table. "I hardly ever see you anymore, you whip in and out of the office so fast these days."

"Well, there's a reason for that, girl. I'm engaged!" she squealed, pulling out her left hand from a leather glove and wriggling it.

"Oh my God! Congratulations, sweetie!" Pauline hugged her, then grabbed her hand and whistled. "*Quel* rock! Our mothers really were right about doctors."

Nic looked at Lou, who roused herself. "Congratulations, hon! You deserve all the best." She hugged Nic and tears welled in her eyes. Not so much because she was happy for Nic—although she was—but because everyone else's life was going so well and hers was going down the toilet.

"Thanks, guys, you're the best. And, Pauline, I want you to know I'm going to be calling you regularly—you, too, Lou—and arranging girls' nights out. I'm not going to be one of those girls who forgets all about her friends."

"So have you planned the wedding?" Pauline asked. "We want to hear all the details!"

"I'm not filming it," Lou announced.

"Of course you're not filming it! You and Pauline are going to be my maids of honor."

"Really?" Now the tears came streaming down Lou's face. "I've never been a maid of honor before."

"I have," Pauline said darkly. "Three times. You're not going to make us wear seafoam green, are you?"

"Of course not! I may be from a small town, but I do know Vera Wang."

"We get to wear Vera?" Lou said excitedly, wiping her face with her hands.

"No, a cheap imitation."

"Good enough."

Nic looked worried. "Pauline, you know what they say—three times a bridesmaid, never a bride. Do you want to back out?"

"Yeah, right, Nic." She reached over, touched her arm and smiled. "It would be a terrific honor to be one of your bridesmaids."

Nic breathed a sigh of relief. "Thanks, Pauline." Now *her* eyes welled up. "It will mean so much to have you guys up there with me. You've been my closest friends since I came to New York. I don't know how I could have gotten used to life here without you guys. Thank you…for all you've done for me."

"Hey," Lou said, wiping an eye. "I thought you said you weren't going to be one of those girls who forgets about her friends. That sounds suspiciously like a farewell speech."

"Gee, can't I say one nice thing?" Nic, busy wiping her own eyes, tried to lighten the mood.

"So, when and where is this shindig going to take place?" Lou asked.

"We haven't finalized anything yet. But it will be fairly small and fairly soon, here in Manhattan."

That surprised Lou. Nic loved the circus weddings they filmed. If the wedding was going to be here, probably only her closest relatives would be coming in.

"Why not in Mayville?"

She shrugged. "My life is here now and Peter and I will be paying the shot. It just seems appropriate that the party celebrating our commitment to each other be here."

Jake materialized like a ghost—all in white, out of *Vogue*'s July issue—beside their table, and said, "Nic is all grown up, Lou. She doesn't need a big, expensive party to celebrate her love for Peter. Congratulations, dear." He hugged Nic while Lou stewed. Hadn't he told her he *liked* circus weddings? Why was he defending Nic? Was he trying to goad Lou into admitting something? That she was pigeonholing people? That seemed to be his theme lately. And he was just so wrong about that! She was about to tell him so when he smiled and said, "I have to go order some java, girls. Have a nice day. Talk to you later, Pauline."

"'Bye, Jake," Pauline said.

Nic looked at Lou worriedly.

She sighed. "I can handle it, guys."

They asked her if she was sure, while glancing at their watches.

"Go," she ordered them, sighing. "Go meet your *men*."

So can *you handle it?* Gigi asked a few moments later, just after Pauline and Nic said their goodbyes.

Handle what?

Handle the fact that Jake may have given up on you.

Just because he's angry with me doesn't mean he's given up on me.

Aha! So you don't want him to give up on you!

I didn't say that!

You implied it.

You're impossible.

You know, Lou, people can surprise you.

Nobody's surprised me yet, Gigi.

You're a tough nut to crack, kiddo....

7

LOU ABANDONED WORK on her screenplay altogether and spent the remainder of the summer working like a fiend on *Hack*, her cinema zine. She begged Pauline to go with her to the Small Press Fair, where she'd taken out a booth. She'd designed the minimagazine on her computer and the photocopied issues looked pretty damned good, she thought. Edgy, but accessible.

The fair was held at a smelly downtown church. Lou had been to the event once before and had had trouble finding it. This time she'd persuaded the reluctant organizers to put a sandwich board on the sidewalk out front. It had taken many a discussion among the egalitarian-minded group before a consensus in favor of this radical idea could be reached. For a bunch of fringe types, Lou thought, they were awfully slow to warm up to new ideas.

She and Pauline checked in with the organizers upon arriving.

"Ah, Lou." A woman with frizzy gray hair smiled frostily at her. "I'm Rita Sandler. We spoke on the phone."

"Oh, Rita! Great to meet you in person, finally. I'm sorry I couldn't make it to—what did you call it?"

Rita smiled tightly again. "Our consensus circle."

"Right. What a great idea. I'm glad it worked."

"Well, it was a very close vote in the end. It would have

helped if you'd been there to make your case." There was a distinct chill in her voice. "As I told you, we had to have several meetings about the sandwich board issue before we could get everyone to feel good about it."

You just had to have a majority of votes, Lou thought, *not get everyone to feel good about it.* "Well, it all worked out in the end," she said brightly. "I'm sure it will bring in more people."

Rita sighed. "I certainly hope so." She checked Lou's name off on her clipboard and stood. "Let me introduce you to Robin." She walked a few steps over to another woman sitting behind the exhibitor badges. Rita cleared her throat. "Robin?"

The other woman looked up, startled. She had wild red hair and equally wild-looking eyes.

Rita smiled. "Sorry, dear. I didn't mean to startle you." She looked at Lou and whispered, "She's very fragile." Lou nodded. Pauline rolled her eyes when Rita wasn't looking.

"Robin, dear, this is Lou. Remember, the zine publisher who had the idea about the sandwich board?"

"That was her?" Robin narrowed her eyes. "You made a lot of people very angry."

Lou didn't quite know what to say about that. "Did I? Gosh, well, I'm sorry about that. I didn't mean for it to be such a big deal. I just thought it would bring in more people—"

"More people?" Robin's eyes got wilder and she began to tug at her hair. "Who wants more people?"

"Now, Robin, calm down," Rita said soothingly, shooting Lou a censorious look. "Lou didn't mean any harm. She meant well. We want more people to see the nice things we write, don't we?"

Robin's eyes were still narrowed and she looked at Lou suspiciously. "I don't know."

"Why don't you give Lou her badge, dear. Then she can take her table and go set up."

"Will she be far away from me?"

"Yes, dear," Rita said reassuringly.

"You made quite the impression here," Pauline whispered in Lou's ear. "Before even meeting them."

Lou sighed. She'd been so sure these were her people.

Maybe they still were, she thought, refusing to be discouraged. They couldn't all be flakes like Rita and Robin.

Could they?

It took Robin a few minutes to calm down enough to find Lou's badge. Then Lou and Pauline had to carry one of the big fold-up tables given to each distributor over to her space.

Once they got there, Pauline unfolded the table and covered it with a white paper tablecloth. Next she picked up a big cardboard sign Lou had hand lettered. "How should I attach this?"

"Tape?" Lou suggested.

Pauline looked at it doubtfully. "I dunno. It's pretty heavy. Do you think tape will hold it?"

Lou shrugged. "It's worth a try."

"So do you have any tape?"

Lou, who was unpacking piles of zines, frowned. "I knew I'd forget something." She glanced to the right of their booth. "I'll go ask her."

She sauntered over to her neighbor's booth, thinking it was probably a good idea to meet some of the other small press people, anyway.

"Hi," she said brightly to the rather severe-looking woman who was unpacking a carton of books.

The woman frowned. "Hello. Can I help you?"

Lou extended her hand. "Lou Bergman. I'm the publisher of *Hack*." She liked how that sounded! "I just wanted to introduce myself—and borrow some tape, if you have any."

The other woman took Lou's hand reluctantly. "Anna Orton," she said. She snatched her hand back after a perfunctory shake.

"Good to meet you, Anna. And your company is—"

"Beggar's Press." She shot Lou an admonishing look. "We publish fiction. *Serious fiction*," she added.

Lou glanced at the books Anna was unloading. There were several copies of something called *And the Tide Pulled Me In*. Lou recalled reading a review of the book in the *Village Voice*. The author had been lauded for her disjointed narrative structure, which Lou didn't think sounded like something she should be lauded for.

"Great review in the *Voice*," she said to Anna.

"Mmm-hmm," the publisher said, not even looking up now.

"So, I don't suppose you have any tape..."

Anna shot her a frosty look. "No."

"Oh. Okay. Well, nice meeting you." *So much for networking.*

She decided to try the booth on the other side, which belonged to a publisher called ArtLife. *Good*, she thought. An artist. Surely an artist—an iconoclast, an outcast—would be a little more sympatico, maybe even take Lou under his or her wing. At the very least, she would get some tape.

"Hi!" Lou said—brightly again—to the lean, black-clad man organizing a series of freestanding shelves that looked as though they'd been custom designed by Karim Rashid. "I'm Lou Bergman, from *Hack*. My booth is next to yours." She extended her hand.

He looked at it, appeared to think about taking it, before

he finally took it and said coolly, "Didn't put in a whole lot of effort, did you?"

She withdrew her hand after he'd shaken it as if she were a leper. "Pardon me?"

He crossed his arms. "Your booth. Just because you're small doesn't mean you have to put your booth together with *tape*."

"How did you do yours?" Lou couldn't help asking.

He tossed his head. "I work in the display industry," he said.

"Ah, so that's—"

"Anyone can do this," he said, shooting her an admonishing look.

"Well, I'm sure it does cost a—"

"Isn't your little magazine worth it?" he said sarcastically.

"Well, of course it's worth it, but—"

"You're not a teenager. Surely you're capable of something a little more professional."

Ouch.

He was right, she realized. But it was too late to do anything about it now. Right now, she just really needed a roll of tape.

"You're absolutely right. Next time," she said. If there was one. "But at the moment, this is all I've got. And I really need some tape. Do you have any?"

He thrust a roll at her in disgust and waved her off.

Instead of saying thank you, she ran.

"Good, lemme have it," Pauline said when she got back to the booth. "I think we're about to open."

Just as a disembodied voice on a megaphone announced that the fair was, in fact, officially open, a young woman walked up to the booth, flipped through a copy of *Hack*, smiled, and said, "Funny. How much?"

Lou, who'd been holding her breath, exhaled. Those were the sweetest words she'd ever heard! "Two bucks," she said.

The woman dug in a pocket of her purple parachute pants, handed Lou two crisp dollar bills, smiled again and said, "Good luck today."

"Thanks," Lou said, smiling back widely. When she had gone, Lou turned to Pauline, who had finally managed to attach the sign to their table, and said in wonderment, "Did you see that?"

Pauline grinned. "I did, indeed."

"You know, this might just work, Pauline! Imagine, I'll be able to work on screenplays while making rent money with _Hack!_"

"Lou, that's two dollars in your hand, not two thousand."

Lou's first customer was quickly followed by another impressed customer, then another and another. While giving change at one point, Lou lifted her head and realized that her booth was the most crowded at the fair. The other publishers were looking longingly in her direction.

"I see you've been doing well today," a familiar voice said.

Oh, God. Lou raised a horrified gaze from the cash box. She'd been right. It was Barbara Laver, her high school nemesis. They'd had to share the Senior English Award _and_ the Senior Theater Arts Award at Long Island High, not to mention an assortment of boyfriends.

Well, they hadn't exactly shared the boyfriends. The truth was, Barb had lured most of them away from Lou. Which hadn't been difficult. Barb had been stunning even then, before she could afford this look—Lou tried not to stare at what she guessed was a five-thousand-dollar rhinoplasty, six-hundred-dollar Manolo Blahniks, a three-hundred-dollar frosting job and a thousand-dollar DKNY suit.

There was no way out. "Barbara! Great to see you!"

"Lou—Lou Bergman?" Barbara gasped. "Oh my God! This is so unbelievable!" To Lou's horror, she reached over to hug her and planted kisses on each of her cheeks, European-style. Then she pulled back and peered at the hand-lettered sign that Lou suddenly realized was hopelessly amateurish.

Barbara cocked an amused—and perfectly sculpted—brow. "So, what, exactly, is *Hack*?" she said in what Lou was sure was a patronizing tone.

Lou mustered a smile. Her brilliant little zine now seemed juvenile and stupid. As did the outfit she'd thrown on in the early morning: a Powerpuff Girls tank top, vintage army pants from the Canal Street Jean Company and a candy-pink hairband.

She laughed. "Oh, *Hack*'s just a fun little something I've been working on, geared to aspiring filmmakers."

"I see." Barbara lifted the eyebrows delicately. "So this is what you're doing now."

"This and about twenty-eight million other things." Lou gave another tinkly little laugh. "Of course, I'm working on a screenplay...." When there was no response from Barbara, she was forced to say, "So, you're a big news personality now, huh?"

Barbara lowered her eyebrows modestly and said, "Well, I don't know if I would say 'big,' exactly."

"And how old is your daughter now?" Lou had heard that Barbara and her rich husband, entrepreneur and man-about-town Jack Lansing, had had a girl a few years ago.

"Vanessa is six and she's already fluent in French and can play Mozart on the violin. Can you believe it? Lou, do you mind if I get a quick spot with you?" Barbara motioned to a young man carrying a camera a few yards away from her. "Lou, this is Gary. Gary, Lou. An old high school friend."

Gary looked at Lou, puzzled. Clearly he thought if she was a high school friend of Barbara's, she was too old to be a zinester.

He's right, Lou thought glumly. Of course, a capital-I Interesting person wouldn't care what people thought.

"Oh, no, Barbara, I don't think I—"

"It'll be fun! Ready? Here goes." Before she knew it, Barbara was talking into her microphone and looking at Gary, who had actually turned his camera on. "Here we are at New York City's semiannual Small Press Fair with Lou Bergman, a dedicated zinester. Tell us a bit about your zine, Lou."

She shoved the microphone in Lou's face. Pauline had just come back from a falafel place down the road with lunch and was giving Lou the thumbs-up sign.

"Actually, Barbara, I'm really a screenwriter. I just put out a fun little zine on the side—called *Hack*—for film buffs and aspiring filmmakers." Suddenly, Lou knew she didn't want *Hack* to be her bread and butter. It would never be a really good-looking publication without bazillions of dollars invested in it. And she didn't want people like Barbara Laver laughing behind her back for the rest of her life.

"So you're publishing for a very specialized audience, then, an audience the mainstream magazines don't reach."

"Yes, but—"

"And how did you do today?"

"Very well. We've just about sold out—"

"I guess people seeking alternative fare know that this is the place to come." Barbara turned to the camera again. "That's the scoop on zines, folks, and that was alternative publisher Lou Bergman, who puts out the teeny-tiny zine

Hack, which fills a small but important niche in the film community. This is Barbara Laver, reporting to you from the Small Press Fair."

She turned back to Lou when the camera was off and said, "Thanks, Lou."

Lou sighed. "No problem."

"So tell me what else you've been up to. Husband? Kids?"

"None of the above," Lou answered, trying to lighten her tone.

"Mmm. So about that screenplay—"

Aha! So she *had* heard!

"—who's your agent?"

Lou could have sworn she saw an evil glint in Barbara's eyes.

"Oh, I'm...still exploring my options."

Barbara lifted her brow again. "I see."

Lou didn't have time to formulate a response to that because in the next moment she saw Barbara's eyes widen and heard her scream, "Jake? Jake Roth?"

JAKE GROANED INWARDLY. Now Barbara Laver was going to corner him and drone on about parties and stock options when all he wanted was to offer Lou support and to apologize for how he'd been behaving recently. Not that he was ready to concede she had a point about his art—he still thought she was dead wrong about that. But he knew he'd been too sensitive on the issue.

And why is that? a little voice in his head asked.

He ignored it.

Barbara was looking expectantly at him. He turned on the charm. "Barbara, you look more gorgeous every day." He pecked her cheek.

"Flatterer! So do you!" She pecked back.

Jake snuck a peek at Lou. He didn't think he imagined that she was staring at his biking gear—or more accurately, at the muscles underneath his biking gear.

"How *are* you?" Barbara exclaimed. "What are you doing here?"

"Great, couldn't be better. I just came by to offer my buddy here some support." He aimed a wide smile at Lou.

"You know Lou?"

Jake didn't like the surprised note in Barbara's voice and moved closer to Lou. "Sure, we're pals, right, kiddo?" Jake said, giving her table—and her—a good once-over. Seeing Pauline, he said, "Hey, cuz."

"Hey to you." Pauline got up from her fold-up chair and extended her hand to Barbara. "I'm Pauline, Lou's friend and Jake's cousin."

"Oh, sorry, guys," Lou said. Jake sensed his presence had flustered her. He was smugly satisfied at the thought. "Pauline, this is my old friend Barbara. Barbara, Pauline."

"Nice to meet you, Pauline," Barbara said. "Well, I've got to be off. Great seeing you, Jake. Will you be at the Black and White Ball on Saturday?"

"Wouldn't miss it."

"Wonderful. See you then." They air-kissed and Barbara left.

Jake didn't miss Lou's sigh of relief.

"So, you know Barbara," he said to her.

"Unfortunately yes."

"Not a big fan, I gather."

"'Will I see you at the Black and White Ball?'" she mimicked.

He lifted his brow. "I've never known you to be catty."

She tossed her head. "Just making an observation."

Jake fingered a copy of *Hack.* "Cute," he said. *Very cute,* he thought. Like Lou herself, the zine looked funny and original. He had to hand it to her. She appeared to have made lemonade out of lemons. "How'd it do today?"

"It did great," she snapped, taking the copy out of his hands and putting it into a carry-all bag with the others.

"Hey, I wanted to buy it," he protested.

"Too late, we're closing—and I'm going out of business."

"I thought this was going to be your life's work," Pauline said.

"*Au contraire*, it's taking too much time away from my screenwriting," she said, suddenly needing to escape. "Sorry to talk and run, guys. I have to—meet someone. Thanks for the help, Pauline. And thanks for coming, Jake."

With that, she took off, leaving the pair of puzzled cousins staring after her.

8

October

PANIC SET IN.

She wasn't going to be a brilliant zine publisher.

She'd abandoned her screenplay.

And her nest egg was dwindling rapidly.

A roommate could help out with the rent.

But she didn't want a roommate who wasn't Pauline or Nic.

It was definitely time to start looking for a new apartment.

"You look pretty focused," Zooey said one bright Sunday morning as she came by the counter Lou was seated at to clear it off. The annoyingly cute couples were out in force, taking up all the good tables.

"I'm trying to keep myself from dwelling on the fact that I'm the biggest personal and professional failure that ever was," Lou said grimly.

Zooey looked at her. "You?"

"Yeah, me."

"But you're so together!"

Lou was mildly encouraged by this. "Me—together?"

"Well, yeah." Zooey snapped her gum and twirled a lock of bright royal-blue hair. "You're so stylish and classy."

Lou was surprised that Zooey thought so. "Stylish and classy?"

Zooey grinned. "Are you going to repeat everything I say?"

"I just thought you thought we were a bunch of old squares."

"God, no, you guys are so cool."

"God, we're so not," Lou said. "*You're* the cool one."

"Well, then, I think I want to be a square."

Lou looked at her and smiled gratefully. "So, any decision on the Taz front yet?"

Zooey sighed. "No. But I'm still thinking about that picket fence."

"I told you, there are no picket fences, just pressure-treated wood ones that—"

"Leach arsenic, I know, I know."

"That's a myth!" Lauren called to them from across the room.

Zooey ignored her. "Hey, where's the rest of your posse?"

"Well, Pauline's off to Martinique for a three-month holiday with her new beau—"

"Three months!"

Lou sighed. "Yeah, I know. She's been stockpiling vacation time for years. Now's a good time to take it 'cuz it's the slow season for weddings. And apparently her doctor honey comes from a sickeningly rich family that actually has a *compound,* not being used at the moment, in Martinique. But Rob's no pampered preppy," she added. "He's going to be working part-time at the local clinic while he's there."

"Wow. A *compound.*" Zooey whistled. "And Nic?"

"Busy as a bee with wedding plans." She circled an ad. "Hey, Zooey, help me out here for a second."

Zooey perched on the stool next to her and peered at the newspaper. "Looking for a new place?"

"Yeah. What do you think about this area?" Lou pointed to the ad.

Zooey looked dubious. "That's the lower East Side."

"Yeah, but that's considered a pretty cool area now, isn't it? Didn't I hear you say you live down there?"

"Yeah, which is why I work here. If I had to be down there twenty-four hours a day, I think I'd go crazy. The charming pickle dealers of old have made way for crack addicts and armed robbers."

"My grandmother still lives there," Sam said from a few stools away. "She won't leave."

"Isn't she terrified?" Zooey asked curiously.

Sam shrugged. "She took some self-defense classes for seniors."

Lou pointed to another ad. "How about that area?"

"Well," Zooey said slowly, "it's further north, but too far east."

Lou remembered her depressing sojourn to the Sacred Squash.

"Yeah, you're right. How 'bout Brooklyn?"

Zooey looked dubious. "Too far from everything."

"And not very classy." Lauren wrinkled her nose as she peered over Lou's shoulder.

"Lotta my truckers live in Brooklyn," Dent said. "Good people."

"They may be good people," Lauren said patiently. "They're just not the *right kind* of people."

"Oh my God, they probably ride bikes every once in a

while," Zee said sarcastically from a table near the entrance.

Lauren smirked. "You sound angrier every time you talk to me, Zee," she said. "Could it be—"

"Don't even say it," he said darkly.

"Brooklyn, people," Lou said. "We're talking about Brooklyn. Isn't it supposed to be getting hipper?"

"I do a lot of filming there," Ingrid said from across the room.

"Hey, where's Ted?" Lauren asked.

Ingrid sighed. "I dumped him when he quit acting to train as a stockbroker."

"Aw, he was nice," Lou said. "Just because he wasn't artsy anymore—"

Everybody looked at her. She cleared her throat and looked back down at the paper. "So, Brooklyn. Hip or not?"

Zooey rolled her eyes. "Please."

"Okay. What about Queens?"

"I have a friend in Queens," Dent said. "Her apartment just got broken into for the ninth time."

"Okay," Lou said. She pointed to another ad. "How about this one?"

"That's more like it," Zooey said approvingly. "Downtown, not too far west, not too far east."

"There must be something wrong with it," Sam said darkly.

"There's no price," Zooey pointed out.

"You'll never be able to afford it," Lauren said scoffingly.

Lou folded up the paper. "Doesn't hurt to check it out."

Check it out she did, about an hour later. It was a charming old brownstone that looked well kept up. Although she suspected Zooey was right and she'd never be able to swing the rent, she knocked at the front door.

"Hi," she said cheerfully when a frazzled-looking woman opened the door. "I'm here about the apartment?"

"Oh!" The woman looked surprised. "Do you...live around here?"

It was a strange question, Lou thought, but she answered anyway.

"No, I've been living on the West Side, midtown, but I've been feeling the downtown itch."

She smiled. "Well, you can't do better than this neighborhood. It's a really nice balance of professionals, students and artists." She held out her hand. "I'm Kay Armstrong. I live and work on the first floor, but as you can see, there's a staircase right here in the entryway for whoever rents out the second floor, so you don't have to ever see me." She smiled and gestured to one side of the foyer, where there was, indeed, a staircase. "Tenants' mailboxes are right here." She pointed to a row of three pretty wrought-iron boxes over the radiator. "Shall we have a look upstairs?"

"I'd love to." Just then Lou noticed the signature on a couple of small paintings on the staircase wall. "You're an artist, Kay?"

"Yes. I have an exhibit in Seattle coming up, so it would be really nice if I could get this settled soon."

The apartment was everything Lou had dreamed of, with soaring ceilings, exquisite moldings, fabulous wood floors and great light—even a working fireplace. The only drawback, she was sure, would be the price.

Lou took a deep breath after the tour. "Kay, I love it. How much are you asking?"

Kay named a ridiculously low monthly figure.

Lou asked her to repeat it.

She repeated it.

"Oh, God, Kay, I know I'm a filmmaker and I realize you probably want someone with a steady job in here, but I give you my solemn word of honor that I'll give you a rent check each and every month, on time and without fail. Please, please, please let me rent this apartment?"

Kay just laughed. "Hey, I'm an artist. It's yours."

Lou screamed and hugged Kay exuberantly. "How soon can I have it?" she asked breathlessly when she finally let Kay go.

Kay shrugged and then she uttered words that, to Lou, seemed to enter the atmosphere sprinkled with fairy dust, "The sooner the better."

I DON'T EVEN NEED to paint, Lou mused one week later, standing in her new living room. The walls were a beautiful, unmarked parchment-white that looked great with the dark wood moldings. Luckily, the bed and dresser she'd shared with Alan were her own, and she'd also kept the crappy old twelve-inch television she'd had in her bedroom as a teenager. She'd brought Aunt Sukie's bridge table and ancient couch, but despite the castoffs, the place looked pretty good by the time she unpacked. Lou's heart soared when she thought about her bright future in the gorgeous new apartment. With the rental fee being so low, she'd soon be able to afford a nice table and couch of her own!

Nice, Gigi commented.

Sure is, Lou thought, satisfied.

More you than the beige place.

Absolutely.

And yet it's not exactly a garret. It's big and beautiful.

What are you getting at?

Well, Lou, it's not exactly the cramped attic starving artists—or aspiring filmmakers—are supposed to live in, is it?

Lou determinedly shut down the voice in her head—which she was becoming more adept at doing—and headed into the bathroom to clean it.

She saw the first one there.

It's true, cockroaches are ugly, was her first thought. Lou had never seen one but she knew instinctively that that was what it was. She screwed up her courage and managed to smash it with a tissue box. *Jeez, those buggers are fast!* she thought. She got a second one the same way.

When she saw the third one, she started to get a little freaked out.

When she saw the fourth roach, she panicked and ran downstairs, out onto the porch. Breathing heavily, she ordered herself to remain calm. And to do up her sweatshirt because it was about a hundred below zero outside. The fall weather had just turned brutal. It was that seasonal moment when all the pretty leaf-changing and "crisp" transitional weather ended and all one had to look forward to was the kind of cold that cut right through to the bone.

What to do? Kay was in Seattle already—and she'd obviously known about the roach problem. That had been the reason, Lou suddenly realized, for the strange "Do you live around here?" question and the rock-bottom rent. Sure, her landlady could afford to ignore the problem; she was away exhibiting her stuff most of the time. She'd probably cleaned and sprayed twice daily to keep the nasty critters at bay while she showed the place.

So where did that leave Lou?

JAKE WAS BIKING over to his friend Ted's house downtown when he saw Lou sitting on a porch. He waved and kept on going, figuring she was visiting some artsy pal. *Or was it a morning-after situation?* He didn't want to think about that. But then he saw her quickly lower her head. He knew instinctively that tears were coursing down her cheeks. In a flash, he was on the driveway, hopping off his bike.

"What is it?" he asked, sitting on the step and putting his arm around her.

"Nothing," she insisted, sniffling.

"C'mon, Lou, it's me."

"You? The same you who twisted my words in front of my friends?"

"It was retaliation, Lou, for your judgment of me."

"I never judged you."

"Let's not relive it, please. Anyway, I came to the Small Press Fair to apologize for that, but you didn't give me a chance. And I stopped just now because I'm concerned." Then it dawned on him. "This is your new place, isn't it? Pauline told me you got a new apartment downtown. Great area."

"Oh? Better than the upper West Side?"

"I didn't say that. Hey, I just want the best for you, kiddo. If you're happy, I'm happy."

She paused. "I'm not entirely happy at the moment."

"I didn't think so."

"There's an army of roaches up there. It's kind of grossing me out."

He nodded. "I used to live in a house near here and I had the same problem."

"What did you do?"

"Found a new place."

She stared at him.

He sighed. "Seriously, Lou, you're gonna have to. They never really go away. Take it from me. You can exterminate till the cows come home. They'll be back in a few days, a few weeks or a few months. Meanwhile you'll be breathing in air that's managed to kill thousands of bugs. If I were you, I'd just swallow the deposit and get the hell out."

He had to be joking! "You just want me to lose the bet."

"Bet, schmet. Sure, I like to win. But I like you, too, and I want you to live a long, healthy, happy life."

Lou stood. "That's sweet, but I don't give up so easily. I'm going back in there."

"I'll go with you."

The two of them sprayed with stuff borrowed from a neighbor, then cleaned until there were no more bug corpses lying around—that they could see, anyway. She thanked him profusely for his help and before he left, he looked her in the eye and said, "If you need me for anything else, just call, Lou. You know you can count on me, right?"

He could see her fighting to keep her eyes from welling up again. Poor thing, he thought. It had been a rough day. "Thanks," was all she could manage to say.

She didn't call him until after she woke up late that night craving a cup of hot cocoa and opened a kitchen cupboard to see about a dozen baby mice and one giant parent feasting on her baking supplies. The story came pouring out when he came back over. Apparently she could handle insects, but not animals with fur and tails.

He couldn't blame her.

"Stay calm, Lou. I have the key to Pauline's place. I'm sure she wouldn't mind if you crashed there for a while. I'll help you get your things together. I have a friend with a storage business who can pick up and store your stuff tomorrow."

He insisted on doing almost everything because the roaches and mice were running rampant and she was severely nauseated. Even he had to fight to keep his disgust at bay.

"Jeez! It's like a Cronenberg movie in here!"

Lou sighed. "Story of my life," she said.

ONCE THEY WERE AT Pauline's, Jake made Lou a mug of tea.

Lou smiled. "Aren't you supposed to be a coffee man?"

He tried to look affronted. "The Havajava serves tea, too, in case you haven't noticed. But even if it didn't, there's a time for coffee—like when you're gossiping with friends—"

"We don't gossip," Lou protested.

"—and a time for tea," he continued, "such as when you've been invaded by roaches and mice."

Lou shuddered. "Don't remind me."

Jake shifted on the couch to stretch his legs. Again, he thought he caught her resting her eyes on his biker pants a couple of seconds too long....

"Thanks for everything today," she said. "Tea included."

He smiled at her. "My pleasure. Well, not a pleasure, exactly. But you know what? This—" he leaned toward her "—is a—"

Lou jumped up off the sofa, spilling her tea. "Ouch! Shoot!"

Jake cursed himself. What the hell had he been thinking? He jumped up, too. "Are you okay?"

"I'm fine—it was just a few drops." She put the tea down on the coffee table. "I just realized what would make me feel so much better...a shower—or a bath. I feel so dirty and—"

"Buggy?" Jake supplied.

"Yeah, I guess that's it," Lou said. "Anyway, I'm sure you wanna get home...."

"No way. I'm going to stay for a while and make sure you're okay. Wouldn't want you to go into shock or anything." He shooed her away. "Go on, take your bath. I'll be a good boy and stay out here."

She sighed. "Thanks."

He'd fully intended to be a good boy—until about a half hour passed without a peep out of her. He headed to the bathroom, knocked lightly on the door and called, "Lou," very softly.

No response.

He tried again, a little louder this time.

Okay, he had no choice. He had to go in.

He opened the door a crack. "Hey, Sleeping Beauty," he said softly.

She'd fallen asleep. But luckily, her head was still resting on the tub ledge. Still, it could easily slide off. He had to wake her up without alarming her, but how?

There was only one way he could think of. He took a

moment to look at her before he woke her. She was so beautiful. He placed his lips tenderly on her cheek....

Her eyes bolted open. "What the hell are you doing!" she shrieked.

Perfect, he thought, disgusted with himself. *Great idea, Roth.* "It was the only way I could think of to wake you up. You're lucky I was here. I saved you from drowning."

"Thanks a bunch." Fully awake now, she had apparently just realized that the bubbles had, for the most part, dissipated. She quickly covered her breasts with her hands. Her face beet-red—not from the steam, he guessed—she said, "Now, shoo. I'm getting out."

He sighed. "I'm shooing, I'm shooing."

When she was dressed—in pj's and a fluffy terry-cloth robe—she came into the living room and, as if nothing had happened, said, "I really am exhausted."

He unfolded himself out of the chair in front of the TV. "You sure you'll be okay? I can sleep on the couch—"

"No," she said quickly. "I'm fine. You've done more than enough already. I spend half my life in Pauline's apartment. It's my second home."

He looked around. "Yeah, well, you'll be comfortable here, anyway." Pauline's apartment was filled with flowers, books, cozy throws, candles and photographs. Jake knew that, despite her practical and sometimes prickly side, his cousin had a very warm, feminine side, as well.

"It's nice," Lou agreed.

"I'm sorry your apartment didn't work out."

"I almost believe you."

He smiled. "You'll find another one."

"I'm sure."

"How much was the rent on that one, anyway?"

She named the figure.

"Pretty low," he commented carefully. "That was a big, beautiful place in a great area."

Lou crossed her arms. "Are you implying that I should have known better? That something had to be wrong with it and I was stupid for not catching on?"

Whoa, backtrack, Jake. "Not at all."

She sighed. "It's okay. I should have known better. Something had to be wrong with it and I was stupid for not catching on."

He grinned. "You may have to set your sights a tad lower, it's true."

She hesitated a moment. "How much lower, do you think?"

He shrugged. "I dunno. Lower East Side?"

"The lower East Side?" she said, incredulous. "Do you know what the lower East Side has become? The charming pickle dealers of old have given way to crack dealers and armed robbers! Do you really want to see me living on the lower East Side?"

"No. I'd hate to see you living on the lower East Side."

"So why did you suggest it?"

No way he'd fall for *that.* "Because you asked."

She peered at him through narrowed eyes and crossed her arms. "It's that damned bet. You're determined to make me think I belong on the upper West Side."

"It's not the bet." Well, it kind of was, but she didn't have to know that. "Weren't we just through this earlier?"

She sighed. She really didn't want to think or to talk about any of this now. All she wanted was to curl up in Pauline's cozy bed.

She frowned. "Hey, this building is so much cuter than my old one. How can Pauline afford it?"

"Are you kidding? Pauline's been investing her money since she was five years old. She could probably afford to rent the Taj Mahal."

"I have savings," Lou said, sighing, "but I can't even afford dinner at an Indian restaurant."

Jake laughed. "Pauline doesn't have a weakness for Juicy Couture T-shirts. She buys Fruit Of The Loom." He smiled when she gave him a look. "A completely understandable extravagance. Juicy makes a great T-shirt. Worth every penny."

"They are," she said defensively.

"That's what I said," he said, still grinning.

"Juicy makes a great T-shirt," she reiterated.

"Right." He saluted. "Okay then. 'Bye."

"'Bye," she said.

He turned to go, but then spun back around.

"I know you have savings, Lou. You wouldn't have undertaken this little experiment if you didn't." He paused. "I think you're very courageous."

"Thanks," was all she said, looking near tears again.

"You're welcome. I'm really going now."

But before leaving, he caught her off guard and planted a tender kiss on her forehead. Then he grinned again and left with a quick, "'Bye."

9

November

IT WAS TIME to get proactive. His next move was bound to earn him some serious points. He'd found out during a phone call from Pauline that Lou was dying to go to El Convento Rino, a hip Latin dance club in a questionable area of town—a place he'd actually been. He planned to whisk her there and impress the pants off of her... hopefully, in the literal as well as the figurative sense, though that was, perhaps, counting his chickens before they hatched.

He couldn't wait to see her face when she realized that Jake the Businessman was the person who was going to introduce her to El Convento Rino....

IT WAS A COOL November night when there was a knock on the door and Lou opened it to a sexy, black-clad Jake, who was grinning. She was glad she'd brushed her hair and was wearing her very best sweats: new pink velour ones she'd picked up at Barney's. Strangely she'd been shopping more, not less, since becoming an avowed antimaterialist and starving artist. She wondered occasionally if her spending binges were the result of inner panic. If they were, spending was a pretty dumb response, since the panic undoubtedly came from watching her nest egg shrink. Although hopefully that would stop soon. She had big news for Jake, but she'd wait for the perfect-perfect moment to share it with him....

"Ever hear of a little device called the telephone?" she said.

"Sure, but if I'd called to invite myself over, you would have said no." He looked around. "Home for the evening?"

Sighing, she gestured him in. "You know what they say—there's no place like home."

Jake grinned evilly. "Do my ears deceive me? Did the capital-I Interesting Lou Bergman really just say 'There's no place like home'?"

"Hey, not fair, it was a throwaway line." She shut the door and flopped down on the sofa. He followed suit. "Anyway, this home is just temporary."

"Somehow I don't think you'll be wanting to do battle with giant insects again soon."

She sighed. "I don't want to. But I'm gonna have to leave when Pauline gets back."

"I'm sure she won't mind you staying with her for a while."

"She probably wouldn't, but I'd feel like a terrible moocher."

"Well, you've done a masterful job of getting off topic," Jake said.

"Which is?" Lou asked suspiciously.

"My wanting to cheer you up by taking you out—" he grinned again "—dancing."

"Excuse me?" Lou said, certain she'd heard wrong.

"Do you like to dance?"

"Well, yeah, but—"

"Then it's perfect. We both like to go dancing." He jumped up from the couch. "Let's go."

"Dancing? Now?"

"Sure. Why not?"

Surely there were a million reasons why she shouldn't go dancing with Jake Roth. But right now she couldn't think of any. Besides, there was that news she was dying to tell him....

She shrugged and stood. "Okay. Lead the way."

Twenty minutes later they were at El Convento Rino, taking a dance lesson. Despite her nonchalant response, Lou was excited about the evening. El Convento Rino was a hip, slightly rundown spot known not only for its dance classes and great Latin music, but its wonderful food. Lou had been hearing about the place for ages. It was pretty ironic, she thought, that Jake the Businessman was the first guy to take her there....

Lou had changed out of her sweats into cargo pants and a chiffon peasant top, going for the casual-but-sexy look. Eliza, their dance instructor, had gone for the out-and-out sexy look, in tight black pants and an equally tight, black wraparound top. Lou snuck a peek at Jake. He didn't appear overly impressed.

"Okay, everyone," Eliza said energetically, "the first thing we need to talk about is hip motion."

Uh-oh, Lou thought. Was she was going to be required to do hip rolls in front of Jake?

She stole another peek at him.

He waggled his eyebrows.

She gulped.

"Let's do more than talk about it, baby," one of the men called out. Everyone laughed. Eliza smiled.

"Funny guy. I'm gonna ask you to demonstrate first if you keep that up." She turned back to the others. "What I'm going to say might surprise you. What's most important to learn is not hip motion, but knee motion."

Phew, Lou thought.

"Once you get the knee motion, good isolated hip motion is the inevitable result."

Uh-oh, Lou thought again.

"So let's get to it. When you want to create a shifting or 'settling' action of the hips, you will bend one knee while leaving the other straight. Watch me."

It was a simple but incredibly sexy motion.

Lou looked at Jake. He looked at her—and held her eyes while he did what Eliza had demonstrated.

Lou gulped yet again.

Jake grinned. "Well, what are you waiting for?"

Lou took a breath and did it.

"Nice," Jake murmured. "Very nice."

Lou didn't know how long she could keep this up without dragging him home, pouncing on him and ripping all his clothes off.

"Good," Eliza said. "Nice work, everybody. Now that you've got that down, let's try a routine. This is your basic cha-cha. Keep all your steps very small. If you don't feel comfortable applying the knee and hip action we just learned, just practice the steps first. Apply the Latin motion as you become capable. Watch me." She started dancing while she reeled off the instructions. "Side step left, rock step back right, recover weight forward left, side step right, step together left. Then side step right, rock step forward left, recover weight back right, side step left, and step together right." She grinned. "Everybody got that?"

"What was the first thing you said?" someone called. More laughter.

"Now it's your turn. Here's the music." She turned a tape machine on and a sexy, pulsating rhythm came on.

Jake was looking at Lou again. He started dancing. Lou nearly fainted, he looked so sexy. She summoned up her courage and began to dance along with him.

"Very nice! This is a talented group," Eliza commented when they were done. "Now, if you want to use these steps as a couples dance, begin in the closed position, with the ladies using opposite footwork." She walked over to Lou and Jake. "You two can demonstrate."

Lou panicked. Dancing in a "closed" position with Jake was bound to upset her already-fragile equilibrium. But everyone was looking at them expectantly. *Suck it up, Lou,* she commanded herself.

She smiled brightly and held her arms out. Jake grinned and took hold of her hands. They started to dance.

Lou thought she would have trouble doing the opposite footwork from Jake, but she didn't. Dancing with Jake, it seemed, was as natural as breathing. Of course, her heart was doing that charming slam dance it always performed when Jake was around, but hopefully she was the only one who heard the rhythmical booming. If she kept smiling and looking calm, no one would suspect a thing....

Everyone whistled and applauded loudly when they were done. Jake smiled widely and gestured toward Lou who curtsied and gestured back toward Jake.

Eliza was smiling. "I wish all my couples caught on so quickly. All right," she said to the others, "you guys ready for more?"

Ready they were. The lesson continued. Lou began to relax and to feel less self-conscious. The music and motion were contagious. She felt free, sexy and more alive than she had in a long time.

"Whew," she said when they sat at a red vinyl-covered booth when the lesson was over. "That was my workout for the week. You don't even look tired. Where do you get the energy?"

"Like all evil businessmen, I work out regularly."

"You belong to a club?"

"Yup."

"I really need to exercise more."

"You're in fine shape, my dear." He waggled his eyebrows lasciviously.

"Thanks—I think. But I felt like a big lump next to some of those dancers. Half of them looked like pros to me. They shouldn't be allowed to come to the lessons. I think we should complain."

He laughed. "Should we order a snack? I think we've earned it."

She sat back in the booth. "Sure. Order whatever's good."

"Done." He gestured a waitress over and gave her their order. The waitress flashed Jake a sexy smile before leaving.

"She likes you," Lou commented.

"Everyone likes me," Jake said.

"Not like you're a cute little puppy dog. She *likes* you."

"Ah. Poor girl. Her affection will remain unrequited."

Lou decided not to ask why. She changed the subject adroitly. "So, come here often?"

He grinned. "Bit late in the game for lines, don't you think?"

"Ha, ha. I'm serious. How long have you been coming here?"

"I used to come here with a bunch of friends from business school."

"Used to?"

"Yeah. You know how it is. You lose touch."

"But you went to business school in New York, didn't you?" she said. "Didn't most of them stay here?"

He shrugged. "Yeah, but their lives are different. Marriage, kids and all that jazz."

She lifted a brow. "You don't strike me as the kind of

person who stops being friends with people just because they get married and have kids. Anyway, didn't you tell me you wanted the whole Long Island shebang?"

"It's not that," he said after a pause. "They changed. Certain businesspeople become myopic, too caught up with making millions, maintaining a lifestyle."

"You make millions and maintain a certain...lifestyle."

He looked at her intensely. "You know, Lou, people can be multifaceted."

What have I been telling you? Gigi whispered in her ear.

"But they usually aren't," Lou said.

"Do you really believe that?" he said. "What about tonight? I surprised you by bringing you here, didn't I?"

"Well, yeah," she admitted.

"So," he said challengingly, "doesn't that prove that you can't put people into little boxes?"

She sighed. "Jake, I just got out of a relationship with a man who was obsessed about making millions and maintaining a certain...lifestyle. Neither he nor his friends were multifaceted and I don't want to live that way."

"No offense, Lou, but you didn't just get out of that relationship. It's been months now. And again, you can't tar all businesspeople with the same brush—that's crazy."

"Well," Lou said, looking at him, "even you can't deny that all businessmen have—secrets."

"Where did you get that idea?"

She hesitated. "It was something Alan said once. I've never forgotten it."

He shook his head. "Alan. Well, guess what, Alan was right—there are plenty of businesspeople who are scumbags. Alan was one of them. But there are plenty of fine, upstanding businesspeople, too."

"But business is all about the bottom line—making the most money you can," Lou insisted. "Isn't there a sort of intrinsic scumminess in that?" Immediately she wondered if she'd gone too far again. Remembering how she'd insulted him when she'd asked him if he was afraid of finding out what the pros thought of his artwork, she tacked on, "No offense."

"None taken." He leaned back in his seat as she breathed an inward sigh of relief. "I make it a point to pay all my Third World coffee suppliers a fair wage by North American standards. If all I was concerned about was the bottom line, I wouldn't do that."

"That's good of you," Lou said, thinking that was *very* good of him.

"It's what everyone should do. I'm nothing special." He paused. "That's not to say I don't have secrets." He leaned forward again. "But I'm not the only person hiding stuff around here."

"What's that supposed to mean?" Lou asked.

"Who's Rona Bernstein?"

Oh, yeah. Lou had forgotten about that.

"You know who she is. You met her. I introduced you."

"And practically threw me out of the restaurant after doing so. And you wouldn't tell me anything about her after she made all those cryptic comments. I repeat, who is Rona Bernstein?"

"Jake, she's an old friend. Period. Can we go back to what we were talking about, please?" She didn't really want to, but she did want to change the subject from Rona. "As I was saying, I'm not putting anybody in a box. I just want to see how the other half lives—not just see it, but live it. Sure, people with millions can hang out at places like these once in a while—" she gestured around them "—and have a ball slumming it. Then they can return to their cavernous homes and take some cold lobster out of the refrigerator."

He looked at her, amused. "Slumming it?"

"That was harsh, I know. Sorry."

He leaned back in his booth. "I do understand, you know."

"You do."

He leaned forward again, took her hands in his and looked at her closely. "I do." He paused. "You know, we have a lot in common when you think about it."

She couldn't breathe. She hoped he'd let go of her hands soon.

He seemed to sense her discomfort and let go.

She exhaled.

He continued. "We're both only children and, whether you realize it or not, I haven't done what everyone expected of me."

"C'mon, Jake. The business world isn't exactly frowned upon," Lou said.

"No," he said, "but the kind of business I eventually started proved a little strange for some of my old pals."

"Why?" Lou asked.

"Think about it, Lou. Do you have any relatives in business?"

"Sure. An uncle and a cousin."

"What kind of businesses are they in?"

She thought for a minute. "My uncle imports and exports. I have no idea what. My cousin has a pool supplies business."

"Exactly. Importing and exporting. Pool supplies. Safe and boring, right?"

Lou shrugged. "I guess."

"I opened a coffee shop with murals on the wall and beat-up garden chairs for seats."

"But it's become huge," Lou protested.

"According to you, maybe. And 'become' is the operative word. I started out not knowing whether it was going to go or be a total flop."

"Really?" Lou asked. It was hard to believe that. Jake seemed the penultimate biz whiz—the next Donald.

"I took a risk," he said, looking pointedly at her.

"So you do believe in risk-taking," she said defensively. "Why discourage me, then?"

"We've been through this," he said.

"Tell me again."

"I'm not out to stop you from doing what you really want to do. It's just that sometimes it's easier for people on the outside to see a situation clearly—"

"I hope you're not saying that you know me better than I know myself...."

"Not at all. But c'mon, Lou, haven't you ever listened to someone moan about, I don't know, her job or her personal life. And you think, if only she could see it, but of course, she can't. You know exactly what she should be doing, but you can't suggest it because that would be patronizing and hurtful. So you stay silent."

"Obviously you've decided to not stay silent," Lou said.

"Right."

"I find your attitude patronizing and hurtful."

He smiled.

"Not to mention hypocritical, seeing as you're such an artsy-fartsy risk-taker yourself, according to the shocking new version of your life story."

Jake laughed. "I'm no artsy-fartsy risk-taker."

"You can say that again. You want **artsy-fartsy** risk-takers, I can introduce you to a few I've met lately." The Learning Annex weekend screenwriting course she'd taken as a refresher recently had been filled with them.

"Hmm. Doesn't sound as if you enjoy their company too much," Jake commented.

"Not true." *Yes, it is.* "I was just trying to make entertaining conversation. There's mean stuff to say about slick businessmen, too. You've heard me say some of it."

"I have and, given that Mr. Slick himself was your last boyfriend, I don't blame you for trying out the artsy-fartsies," Jake said generously.

"Glad to hear it."

"But after you're done trying them out, you'll come back to us money-grubbing plebes on the upper West Side."

Lou raised a brow. "I don't think you qualify as a plebe."

"What *is* a plebe, anyway?"

"It's short for plebeian, meaning a Roman commoner."

"Really? Gee, it's fun to go out with a screenwriter."

"Aha! You called me a screenwriter!"

"Slip of the tongue, m'dear. Slip of the tongue."

Lou laughed. "I think not." She paused dramatically. It was time. "I've landed myself an agent, you know."

He looked at her askance. She smiled widely. At the end of October, her block had finally ended. She'd finished *Capra Girl* in a rush of inspiration and sent it off to Paul Jones, a local agent who just happened to have attended Long Island High at the same time Lou had. She'd been dying to tell somebody her news—she'd gotten the call from Paul, who'd agreed to take her on as a client, just an hour before Jake had shown up and hadn't been able to reach anyone.

"You did? Why didn't you tell me? I would have made a toast! Congratulations!"

She looked at him suspiciously. "Hmm. You sound sincere enough…"

"Well, your screenplay must be pretty fantastic for an agent to take it on. I didn't even know you'd finished it!"

She shrugged, trying to remain casual. "I finished it a

couple of weeks ago and found out that an old acquaintance from high school works as an agent now." Paul had palled around with Perry Moss at Long Island High. She was sure the news about her screenplay would reach Perry and the thought was extremely satisfying. "He thinks enough of it to send it around to producers, but until it sells," she added modestly, " I can't really crow about success."

"Still, landing an agent is pretty tough, from what I hear."

Lou was amused. "From what you hear?"

"I have a couple of friends in the business."

"You do? Who?"

"Bill Blake. Howard Philips."

Lou stared at him. "You know Bill Blake and Howard Philips?" They were the hottest Broadway producers in New York.

"Yeah. For ages. They invested in the Havajava."

Lou couldn't believe it. The Havajava wasn't faux artsy, after all: real artsies were connected with it!

Just then, the sexy waitress brought their food. "Enjoy," she said, looking straight at Jake, who smiled at her.

"Oh, we will," he said.

"You didn't have to answer like *that*," Lou said once the waitress had gone.

"Like what?" he said innocently.

"Like you—want her or something."

"You think I want her?"

"I'm sure I don't know," Lou said primly. "And I don't want to know."

He smiled. "I wonder why."

Lou took a closer look at the food. "Mmm, shrimp. How did you know I loved shrimp?"

Before she knew it, he had plucked a shrimp out of the

ice-filled glass, dipped it into some cocktail sauce and was holding it near her mouth.

She gulped—before eating. Did he really expect her to eat it out of his hands?

"Go ahead. I guarantee you'll think you've died and gone to heaven."

She willed herself not to hyperventilate and took a teensy bite off the end.

He shook his head and looked at her intensely. "Not good enough."

"You—you're right. It's delicious."

"So you want more?"

"Y-yes," she said. Oh, God, how had she become trapped in an erotic dialogue?

"Then take more," he said, his eyes never leaving her face.

She closed her eyes and virtually snapped up the remaining shrimp, trying to ignore the heat she felt in her nether regions as her lips touched his fingers.

"Good, isn't it," he said, smiling widely.

"So good I'm putting a few more on to my plate," she said, glaring at him. Damned if he was going to have her eating out of his hands all night.

He leaned back in the booth. "I'm glad I brought you here," he said, watching her eat.

"I'm glad, too," she said as lightly as she could between bites of shrimp. She'd never felt self-conscious eating in front of Jake before—she did it all the time at the Havajava—but something between them had changed here at El Convento Rino....

When she'd finished her shrimp, he cupped a hand to his ear. "Hear that?"

"Hear what?"

"The song they're playing. A ballad. You can't be too tired to slow dance."

Slow dance. He wanted her to slow dance.

"Oh, I really don't th—"

"C'mon." He was up and at her side, holding a hand out and grinning winningly. The sexy waitress was looking at her contemptuously.

She sighed. "Oh, all right."

"Tell me you don't love this song," he said on the way to the dance floor.

"I do love this song," she admitted.

"I knew it," he murmured, bringing her body close to his and holding her tight in his strong embrace.

Breathe, she commanded herself. Which was probably a mistake, because when she breathed, she couldn't avoid but take in his undeniably masculine scent.

"Relax," he murmured.

She couldn't fight him any longer. She put her head down on his shoulder and closed her eyes.

"This is nice," he said softly.

"Yeah," she said.

Too nice, she thought. *One dance*, she told herself. What was one dance?

The answer came to her immediately. Enough to confuse the hell out of her.

10

December

THAT WAS IT, Lou vowed after her night out with Jake. No more erotic shrimp feedings, no more close dances. She'd practically run into her apartment when Jake had dropped her off. She was determined to maintain the status quo. She couldn't—wouldn't—let him distract her from her quest, though remaining undistracted was becoming increasingly difficult.

Which reminded her that the search for inner peace was a major component of any quest. She certainly hadn't been doing a very good job in the relaxation department, Lou thought, suddenly determined to make herself a more centered person. Now that she'd landed an agent, she could afford to take a short rest and concentrate for a while on her inner self. But she definitely needed help from the pros.

And so it was that one day in December, at a New Age bookstore downtown, she dutifully stocked up on some titles, though most of the ones she ended up coming home with had more to do with finding a suitable romantic partner than achieving inner peace.

The first opus was written by the current guru to stars with one name. A quick skim revealed that Bodhi—he, too, had only one name—was less interested in the eastern philosophies he claimed to hold dear than in standard western—i.e., Californian New Age-y—crap. He had a very complicated system of figuring out one's aura color and matching it to a complimentary aura color.

Auras, the voice in her head said scoffingly. *Strictly for amateurs. You still don't see it, do you?*

Hello, Gigi. And how are you?

Hello, Lou. I'm fine, thank you. I don't need to ask you how you are because I've been watching you for months now and I've seen how all your little experiments have turned out. What I've seen is that you haven't enjoyed anything you tried on your own—except for creating me, of course—but you have enjoyed everything that Jake's introduced you to.

But I've only just scratched the surface. I haven't done half the things I want to try. And I've told you a million times, I'm not willing to start something with Jake. You've told me I don't listen to my heart. Maybe not, but I am listening to something inside me—something telling me it's not the right time. Maybe it's my brain I'm listening to rather than my heart, but right now, that's what's speaking louder to me.

She forced her attention back to the pile of self-help books, grabbing one of those You-are-like-the-she-wolf type things. Reading between the lines, Lou deduced that the she-wolf who wrote the thing thought that the she-wolves reading the thing should mate not with he-wolves, but with other she-wolves, which wasn't Lou's cup of tea, though she cared not a whit if other she-wolves felt that particular urge. And so it was on to another book.

Which put forth an interesting theory about one's physical condition being inexorably linked to one's inner state. The author, a blond Californian, was particularly enthusiastic about yoga as a "system of refining the body, the mind and the spirit in unison, ultimately leading to well-being, peace and bliss."

Which sounded pretty good to Lou, so she decided to

join a gym. Exercise would get the old endorphins going and help her feel better about herself. And there was always the chance of meeting an interesting man—an actor or something—at one of those funky clubs downtown that featured yoga and African movement classes....

Later that evening, the enthusiastic young receptionist at Ska on 21st Street raved about the yoga class. Roni was a devotee herself—of the class and the teacher. "Anselma is so great," she enthused, "so balanced and centered. You'll love her."

Lou wasn't so sure, but took a spot in the yoga room, anyway. Soon, Anselma—a hippie type whose hair was done up in cornrows—walked in as if she were the Maharishi herself, slowly and smiling.

The room was silent.

"Welcome, newcomers," Anselma said, her eyes lighting on Lou's briefly. "Through the study of yoga we develop qualities such as fitness, discipline and confidence, but we also become more aware and intuitive, ultimately more stable and contented. One develops a natural high, so to speak, one that is very different from the feeling one gets as a result of being addicted to harmful substances."

Why wasn't the whole world taking up yoga? Lou wondered. She allowed herself to become a little excited. Was this it? Was this the key to getting rid of her lingering interest in material things? She had used the possible screenplay sale as an excuse for going wild in various shops around town. She knew she had to start reining herself in again.

"We will now do our asanas," Anselma continued. "Our yoga exercises, for the newcomers to the class. Relax, breathe slowly and deeply through your nose and just go with the flow. Don't force yourself into any position for longer than it feels comfortable. This will help you conserve your prana."

Piranha? Lou thought.

"Prana is energy," Anselma said.

Oh, Lou thought.

"Do not try and control your thoughts, but do try to focus your awareness on your breathing and your body. Eventually you will be able to enter a state of complete relaxation and oneness while doing your asanas. In time, you may want to add a mantra. Let us begin with the Perfect pose."

Despite Anselma's confusing instructions—"Press the *mulud haru cakra* with your left heel, then press the *svadhisthama cakra* with your right heel..."—this turned out to be a simple cross-legged position.

Piece of cake, Lou thought. She sat straight, held the pose and breathed.

"Now, the Bellows pose."

In this position, Anselma's students were on their backs, knees bent and brought up to their chests. Knees were grasped with hands.

It was almost too easy, Lou thought.

Ditto for the Cobra, which required one to start on one's stomach. One then raised one's chest, palms on the floor and rolled one's head and neck to look up toward the ceiling.

The Head-to-Knee pose was slightly more problematic. Anselma began by sitting with her legs stretched out. She bent her right knee, keeping the knee on the floor, so that she touched the *muladhara cakra*—her left thigh, Lou observed—with her right heel and then she touched her left knee with her forehead.

Most of the others, Lou noted, were able to extend their

backs as elegantly and gracefully over their legs as Anselma.

Lou had to hunch hers unattractively to get her head anywhere near her knee.

She became very excited when Anselma mentioned the Lotus pose. The classic, famous yoga position!

It started out like the Perfect Pose they'd begun with.

The added complication in the Lotus was that both feet were brought up onto the opposite knees.

Lou toppled over not once, but twice, trying to master the position.

Once she got it, she breathed in deeply and, as she was doing so, let loose the loudest burp ever.

The other students stared. Anselma looked at her as if to reprimand her for breaking the beautiful silence.

Lou felt herself turn beet-red.

The red turned to blue when she attempted the Wheel pose—the classic "bridge" that she'd tried, unsuccessfully, to master all through elementary school.

It hadn't gotten any easier.

She didn't even try the Bow pose in which, from a prone position, one was required to bend one's knees and reach behind to grasp one's ankles, then one raised one's head, chest and legs, supporting one's weight on one's navel.

And she could only stare in amazement as the rest of the class did the Locust, going from a face-to-the-floor position to raise their chins, then their legs and their waists up into the air.

Enough of this. Lou took a quick, possibly record-setting, shower. But before getting the hell out of the club—never to return again, she vowed—she decided to treat herself to a massage. Not a full-body massage, but a reflexology massage. Which was, Roni the receptionist told her cheerfully, a fancy way of saying foot massage.

As soon as she was shown into the reflexology room, she regretted her hasty decision.

Relax, she ordered herself, even though the music—some Yanni-ish sitar-based thing—and the sickeningly sweet smell were really getting to her. Aromatherapy, she decided, was something else that was highly overrated.

Roni smiled and said, "Just slip your socks off and hop onto the table. Mika will be with you in a few minutes."

When the door opened a moment later, a man walked in. A man who also sported cornrows and wore a damp Guatemalan wool shirt that smelled of, well, wet Guatemalan wool.

"Hey." He smiled serenely at her and extended his hand. "I'm Mika."

She shook his hand

"Ever had a reflexology massage before?" he asked with a glint in his eye and she panicked for a moment, hoping she wasn't in for some form of granola head torture.

She didn't need to worry. The foot massage itself was not unpleasant. What was unpleasant was the overenthusiastic stream of inane psychobabble Mika kept up through the process.

When he said, "This area here is great for the spleen," Lou lost it.

"You're massaging my foot. How can you be helping my spleen?" she exploded. She didn't even know where her spleen was, but she knew it wasn't anywhere near her foot.

"Your whole body is connected." Mika grinned. "Relax. Let go of your anger."

Lou jumped off the table. "You know what? I can't relax. I had a really bad time today, the smell in here is making me sick and you know what else? Sometimes I just don't want to let go of my anger."

"Try a fish tank," the reflexologist called after her as she stormed out. "Great for easing stress!"

WAS THAT LOU STORMING OUT of the reflexologist's office? Jake wondered. He got his answer a moment later.

"Ouch," he said, grinning when she crashed into him. Ooh, he could have fun with this. "Flaky New Age foot guy got to you, huh?"

She stared at him. "What are you doing here?"

"This is my club," he said.

"You work out—here?" she said dumbly.

"Yeah, I like the people, the downtown vibe." He shook his head, still grinning. He couldn't believe this stroke of luck! "You've really got to stop putting people in boxes, Lou." He moved closer. "Hmm, we had a great time dancing and we work out at the same club. Could it be that some sellouts aren't as bad as you thought?"

"Jake, why are you always confusing the issue?"

"Why do you always make the issue so confusing?" He gestured toward the juice bar. "Juice?"

She shrugged and sighed. "Why not?"

Jake ordered a fresh-squeezed grapefruit; Lou, an orange juice.

When they sat, she said darkly, "I see you're not too far gone—you didn't add wheat grass or protein powder."

Jake lifted a brow. "Now, Lou, you're not making fun of health enthusiasts, are you?"

"Wouldn't dream of it," she muttered, staring daggers at a dancer type at the bar.

"Because, you know, that would be very hypocritical of you."

"Yeah, I got your point," she said, turning her lethal glare on Jake.

"Lemme guess—you were doing yoga, right?"

She nodded dispiritedly.

He grinned. "Hey, don't look so glum. It took me ages to get the poses down. You can't just walk into a yoga class and expect to be an expert right off the bat."

She stared. "You do yoga?"

He wagged a finger at her. "Now there you go putting people into boxes again, Lou. What did you think? That all I do to keep fit is play basketball with my rich pals?"

"Something like that," she muttered.

"Well, I do love to play basketball with my rich pals. I do it once a week."

She rolled her eyes. "Naturally."

He smiled. "If it's any consolation, you look very fetching in your yoga duds."

Her face reddened. "Thanks," she said.

"Everyone and his brother is coming out with a yoga line these days," Jake commented. "And the stuff isn't cheap."

"Let me guess. You're implying that I'm not a true bohemian because I have money to spend on Toula yoga outfits."

"*Moi?* I wouldn't dream of implying such a thing." He sipped his juice. "So, any news from your agent? Any interest from producers?"

"Nope."

"Not to worry. I'm sure you'll hear something soon."

She sighed. "Yeah."

For some reason, he didn't want to remind her she'd probably be better off with a steady job. "So," he said, "how are things at Pauline's?"

"Fine," Lou said curtly.

"Like it there, do you?"

She glared again. "It's okay for now."

"My, what big teeth you have, Grandma. A little stressed out, are we?"

"Apparently," she said grumpily. "Wasn't the yoga supposed to take care of that?"

"Rome wasn't built in a day, m'dear. But yoga's not for everybody. Did you try it more for the exercise or for the spiritual component?"

She shrugged. "Both, I guess. More for the—peacefulness it's supposed to bring you."

Jake realized she probably felt awkward discussing this with him. She was virtually admitting that she was a mess. Again, he decided not to take advantage. "Well, maybe the flaky boho reflexologist was on to something."

"You mean about the fish tank?" Lou asked. "You heard that, huh?"

"I think the whole city heard that. You know, I have a tank upstairs in my office. Did you know there have actually been studies done proving that the sound of running water is so soothing, it makes your body release endorphins? Being around animals does the same thing."

"Petting dogs and cats, maybe," Lou said dubiously. "But a fish tank? I don't buy it."

He shrugged. "So get a dog or cat."

"Can't while I'm at Pauline's. Besides, I have no idea what's in store for me in the future. I don't know where I'll be living and I might not be working at home. It wouldn't be fair."

"Ready to do battle with insects and furry creatures again, are you?"

"I'm sure not *all* non-upper West Side apartments have insects and furry creatures, Jake."

"You'd be surprised, Lou."

She'd finished her orange juice and stood. Apparently he'd pushed too hard. "Goodbye, Jake."

"Goodbye, Lou."

WHEN NIC CAME BY Pauline's apartment that evening, she found Lou smiling blissfully at a goldfish bowl.

"What's that?" she asked suspiciously.

"Goldfish," Lou said beatifically. "Aren't they beautiful?"

Nic looked at them, then back at Lou. "How did it go at the gym?"

"The reflexologist suggested I get these fish. He said they were great for stress. And you know what? He was right. I could stare at these guys all day."

Nic looked at the bowl doubtfully. "Honey, I'm pretty sure he meant a big tank. I think watching two fish chasing each other around in a tiny bowl might have the opposite effect—make you crazy."

Lou smiled. "These guys don't chase each other. Look at them! They look so content. You know, Nic, there's another reason I bought the fish. Do you know I've never had a pet in my entire life? I've only had these guys for a couple of hours, but already I really care about them! What a fantastic feeling! Maybe I'm the Earth Mother type! Maybe I should have a jillion kids! Who needs a man?" She leaned forward and smiled indulgently at the fish. "These guys could be my practice children. You know, Nic, I always thought I was too self-absorbed to be a good parent. But tonight, I found out that I'm a terrific parent—completely giving!" She giggled. "I was supposed to give them a few flakes of fish food, but I've given them half the box! Hey, why did that one flip over like that? Why does he look so—strange? And now the other one's doing the same thing...."

Nic put a gentle hand on her shoulder. "Honey, I hate to break it to you, but I think you've just gone and killed your practice children."

After flushing the kids down the toilet, Nic arranged for Lou to baby-sit her neighbor's five-year-old that night, insisting that she had to get back in the nurturing saddle. Unfortunately, little Madison turned out to hate Lou enough to tell her mother that Lou had spent the entire evening on the phone—which she hadn't.

She was a flop at the mind-body thing, Lou concluded, and a lousy giver-nurturer, to boot.

Despite working on her inner self, the inner Lou, it seemed, couldn't really be helped.

11

Still December

"THAT WAS THE SCARIEST thing I've ever done," Nic stated a couple of nights later as she sat at a table in the new S-and-M-themed restaurant Lou had dragged her to because she was desperate to rebel somewhere she wouldn't bump into Jake. She was desperate to rebel period. Months had gone by since she'd made that stupid bet and, despite all her efforts to change her life, it was barely any different from the one she'd had before making the bet—except for the fact that she was significantly poorer. Panicked about her seeming inability to make even the slightest alteration in her life, she'd enlisted Nic for a wild night out on the town. She was going to have an adventure if it killed her.

And it just might, she thought, sighing. Nic was right. Their little journey to the restaurant hadn't been a whole lot of fun. They'd taken the subway to the lower East Side, then walked over to the restaurant. On the way, Lou discovered for herself that the charming pickle pedlars had, indeed, given way to vicious crack dealers.

But she wasn't about to give up. Nosirree. Nor was she about to let Nic drag her down. "Relax," she said. "We're alive aren't we?" She looked around, knitting her eyebrows. "It's disappointingly tame, don't you think?" The waiters and waitresses were outfitted in black leather and there were whips hung on the blood-red walls, but the patrons looked like the same sophisticated baby boomers who could be found at any new upscale eatery on the middle or upper East or West side.

"Hello, I'm Richard. Feel free to boss me around this evening," their waiter said coquettishly as he appeared at their table and handed them their menus. Richard was shirtless and sported a nipple ring. "Our specials tonight are Bloody Beef Tenderloin, Hot and Spicy Meatloaf and Crack-Me-Open Mussels."

Nic's jaw dropped and she put a hand on her chest. Inexplicably she'd dressed for a tea party at Buckingham Palace wearing a white skirt and one of her stewardess blazers.

"Any questions?" Richard asked.

"You'll have to give us a minute to look at the menu," Lou said, "but I do want to ask you one question right now," she added conspiratorially.

"Shoot."

"Did you have to get that nipple ring for the job?" she asked, winking.

"Lou!" Nic gasped.

Richard grinned. "Nah. Already had it." He leaned toward them. "I'm a regular at Club X in Alphabet City. The real deal." He straightened. "I'll be back in two to take your order."

When he left, Lou's eyes were gleaming.

"No, Lou, absolutely not," Nic said. "We are not going—"

"Aw, c'mon, Nic. We'll have dinner here, but let's go check out Club X after. Aren't you even a wee bit curious?"

"No," she said.

Lou pulled her trump card. "Nic, sooner or later you've

got to see the seamier parts of New York or you'll never be able to call yourself a proper New Yorker."

Nic was about to answer, but just then Lou suddenly started doing a strange, in-her-seat dance. "What on earth are you doing?" she asked.

"It's this bustier," Lou said, trying to adjust it surreptitiously. "It's so damn itchy."

"I told you not to buy it," Nic said admonishingly.

"But it was so perfect for tonight...."

Nic looked around. "Yes, I'm sure you're really happy you invested a hundred bucks for what looks like a gimmicky tourist trap with mediocre food, when you can barely afford rent."

"I can, too, afford rent," Lou said defensively. Nic's outburst had shocked her a little—she almost sounded like a real New Yorker. When had her friend started being able to differentiate between real restaurants and tourist traps? And when had the sarcasm begun to creep in? "I just can't deal with looking at new apartments yet," she added finally. Especially at the kind of apartments she could afford. Her nest egg was now officially puny. And the temporary euphoria she'd felt upon landing an agent had long dissipated. She still hadn't heard from Paul.

Richard returned and they ordered. Lou went with the mussels and Nic the beef tenderloin.

When he left Lou said, "So, how go the wedding plans?"

"Good," Nic said quickly.

"What's his family like?" Lou asked. "Are they nice?"

"Yeah, they're nice. Parents, a couple of younger brothers. All nice."

"What's wrong?" Lou asked suspiciously.

"Nothing. Why?"

Lou looked at her. Something wasn't right. "The parents really okay?"

"Yup. They love me."

Just then, Richard brought their food.

"That was fast," Lou commented.

Richard leaned toward them. "They prepare the food ahead of time."

"It tastes like it," Nic said a moment later, chewing her beef.

"Okay, what have you done with my friend Nic, bitch?" Lou asked, throwing down the cracker she'd been given for her mussels.

She sighed. "I'm sorry, Lou. I guess it's the stress of planning a wedding. It's getting to me. Can we please not talk about it anymore?"

"Sure, hon." Lou spit out a mussel. "God, this is awful."

"Can't compare to Steakfrites, can it?" Nic shrugged when Lou stared at her. "Pauline told me you went there with Jake a while ago. How was it?"

"It was all right."

"Just all right?" Nic asked. "Peter wants to take my family there when they come in for the wedding. Everyone says it's the best steak place in town."

Lou shrugged. "It beats that, I'm sure." She gestured to the tenderloin Nic had abandoned. Both of them were chewing on stale bread now.

"So how's Jake doing, anyway?"

Lou looked at her, eyes narrowed. "You sound coy."

"What?"

"You think something's going on between me and Jake," she said accusingly.

"Well, Lou, you guys have sure been seeing a lot of each other outside the Havajava—"

"Four times! We've seen each other *four* times! And only because of that damned bet. Either he's dragging me places I think I'll like but end up hating, just to prove his point, or he's taking me places I think I'll hate but end up liking—"

"Yeah, sure, whatever you say, hon."

Lou threw her napkin on the table. "Let's get out of here." She wasn't eating, anyway, and she had to get Nic off the topic of Jake. She looked around for Richard, whom she soon spotted at a corner table, angrily whispering to a very scary-looking man sitting at a table near the back.

The scary-looking man was saying something to Richard, who was trembling.

Lou nudged Nic. "Look, I bet that's Richard's partner."

Nic looked. "Pathetic," she said.

"I guess they get something from each other," Lou said, shrugging. "One needs to dominate and the other needs to submit."

"Shouldn't all partnerships be equal?"

"Well, of course I think so and you think so," Lou said patiently, "but Nic, we really shouldn't sit in judgment of others. People have all kinds of passions and preferences in this world."

"Oh, God!" Nic screeched. "He's pulling out a knife!"

Lou smiled. "Relax. It's probably one of their little games."

"He's pulling out another one!"

Lou rolled her eyes. "I'll go over just to make you feel better."

"What? Lou, are you crazy! Lou, get back here—"

"Hey, Richard," Lou said smoothly as she walked up to the table he was standing beside. "We're ready for the check anytime."

"What's her problem?" the man said to Richard.

"You'd better go sit down," Richard whispered to Lou. He was pale and shaky.

"Okay, sure." She turned a bright smile on the man

seated at the table. "You look like a Club X regular. I'm thinking of going there later."

The man grinned at her. "That so?"

"Yup. Richard recommended it."

The man looked back at Richard. "Really now."

Richard gulped. "Actually, I've never been. I just wanted to make her think I'd been there—"

"What? You've never been? Then why did you say—don't you two know each other from there?"

Richard glared at her. "I've never met this man before in my life."

The stranger grinned at Lou. "This is what you call a standard-issue holdup. I was just asking Richard here to get me some money from the cash. Figured people wouldn't take much notice of a scary-looking dude in here. After all, you uptowners are coming here for a little excitement, right? Now, don't you move, missy, and you won't get hurt."

"But my friend—" she looked helplessly at Nic.

The scary-looking man waved at her.

Nic waved back.

Lou straightened and turned back to the scary-looking man. As she did so, she mimed punching a number on her cell phone with her hands behind her back, knowing that Nic would never be able to figure out what the hell she was doing. "Look, this is silly," she said as she continued to mime. "Leave Richard alone." When she'd finished miming, she took her purse off her shoulder. "Here's my purse." She thrust it at him. "Take what you want."

"Well now, that's awfully nice of you." He threw back her purse. "But I'm kinda havin' fun tormenting Richard here."

Lou told herself to keep talking to him. Hopefully, Nic had gotten the hint and had called the police.

"It's not nice to bully people," she said as firmly as she could, despite the fact that she was terrified.

"It's not nice to bully people," the robber said in a falsetto voice. "Hell, where were you born?"

Lou crossed her arms. "Right here in New York."

"Yeah? What part of New York?"

Lou paused. "Long Island."

"Long Island!" He laughed. "That don't count."

"It counts where I come from," a man said smoothly, slipping handcuffs on the scary-looking guy's wrists before he could even clap his eyes on the man.

Lou turned back to Nic, who held up her cell phone. Lou breathed a sigh of relief and gave her the thumbs up. Then she turned back to the plainclothes police officer. "How did you get here so fast?"

"Station's just down the block." He turned to the man he'd just cuffed. "C'mon, Johnny." He yanked him up.

"But I wasn't doin' nuthin'," Johnny whined. "Just makin' conversation."

"He pulled a knife," Richard, now composed, said huffily.

"And he told me he asked Richard to get money," Lou added.

"That's enough for me. C'mon, everybody, we're goin' to the station."

"Me, too?" Lou asked.

"Course you, too. You have to make a statement."

"Oh, I can't go home?" Now that it was sinking in that she'd actually been part of a real-life, honest-to-God robbery, life down here in the capital-I Interesting lower East Side suddenly didn't feel so exciting.

She sighed. It was one more point in favor of the argument that she might not, in fact, be cut out for a capital-I Interesting life. It was a depressing thought. Heck, even Jake was turning out to be more wild and artsy than her, what with his yoga classes at Ska and so forth.

The cop rolled his eyes. "What part of 'you have to make a statement' didn't you understand?"

"Just a second—I have to let my friend know." She headed back over to Nic, who exclaimed, "Jeez! Are you okay? Let's get out of here—"

"I have to go to the station first," Lou said tiredly. "It's just down the block."

"Oh, right. I guess you have to give a statement or something. Don't worry," she said soothingly, patting Lou's arm. "It'll be over soon, I'm sure."

She certainly hoped so, Lou thought, disgusted with herself.

A COUPLE OF HOURS LATER they were finally able to leave the station. Lou decided she wanted to give the wild life one more chance. "You know," she said hopefully to Nic, "it's still pretty early. We could hit a bar or something. I've always hated bars, but maybe I've gotta be a little more adventurous. Who's to say I won't find Mr. Right in a bar? Or Ms. Right, for that matter! Do you realize, Nic, I've always just assumed I was a heterosexual. Why? Why have I never even *considered* that I may not be straight?"

"Because you've never been attracted to women?" Nic said.

Lou ignored her, pulling Nic into the bar, which, serendipitously, turned out to be a gay women's establishment.

"We're in luck!" she squealed, dragging Nic over to the crowded counter area, where she managed to score two stools and order a pair of litchi martinis.

"Now we're in trouble," Nic said as a few pairs of eyes, then legs, came toward them.

"You're new here," an attractive blonde in a slinky red dress commented, slipping onto a bar stool next to Lou, who had already downed most of her martini.

"Sure am," she said, slurring her words slightly. She'd barely eaten and had made her drink disappear in fairly short order. "I'm being reborn."

"And your friend?" the blonde said. "Is she being reborn along with you?"

Lou grinned and turned to Nic, on her other side. "Hey, Nic, she thinks we're together!"

"We're not together," Nic said grimly.

"Great," said the blonde. She turned to her. "I'm Lynn. Can I buy you a drink?"

"Thanks a bunch, Lynn. But you know, I'm a cheap drunk. I think I've had enough to drink."

"I quite agree," Nic said.

"Okay. How about some nacho chips or something?"

"Didja hear that, Nic?" Lou squealed. "Nacho chips!"

"Some nacho chips for the lady," Lynn told the bartender.

Nic sighed.

"So, you haven't told me your name," Lynn said.

"It's Lou. Short for Louise."

"Lou. I like it."

"Cuz it's butch, right? If we were a couple, you'd be the girl. But what if I wanted to be the girl?" Lou was vaguely aware that she was being silly, but she couldn't seem to stop herself.

"You could be the girl." Lynn looked highly amused.

"Is there always a girl and a boy?"

"No, there are always two girls."

"Well, duh. I mean a butch half and a femme half." Lou

was very proud of herself for knowing the terms. "I just finished reading *She-Wolf*. Very enlightening." She'd skimmed it and quickly rejected it, but she felt proud that she'd even bought it.

Lynn was still looking amused. "It isn't always that way."

"Oh."

Just then Lou realized she didn't want to be a femme or a butch—or eat any nacho chips, as she was feeling vaguely queasy.

She sighed. "Lynn, you seem really nice, but I think I've made a mistake." She grabbed Nic by the elbow. "Come on. Let's get out of here."

"Where are we going now?" Nic said once they were outside and Lou was dragging her across the street.

"This place across the road."

"What?" Nic screeched as she read the sign. "Lou, are you *crazy*?"

"Yes! Maybe I'm not crazy enough, Nic! I *wanna* be crazy tonight!"

"Lou, this is a tattoo parlor!"

"They do piercings, too."

"Oh." Nic was relieved. "So what are you going to do— get another hole in your ear?"

"No, silly. I'm going to pierce my lip or something." She swung the door open and pulled Nic through.

"Oh, no, you're not! I won't let you!"

"You ca-an't stop me!" Lou started dancing around her, stopping only when the Hell's Angel-type proprietor came out to the front counter from the back room.

"What can I do for you ladies?" He looked at them suspiciously.

"Not me," Nic said. "Her." She crossed her arms, as if to challenge Lou.

Lou stuck out her bottom lip defiantly. "I'd like a lip ring, please."

"Lou, no."

"Relax, Nic. Everybody's doing it, am I right?" Lou said to the Angel.

"Well, not quite everybody," he admitted, picking up what looked suspiciously like a staple gun.

In no time, the deed was done and Nic and Lou were back on the West Side, sitting in Charlie Z's, a bar that Nic hadn't wanted to go into as it was one of the few left that hadn't been yuppified for the investment banker crowd. But neither had she wanted to leave Lou alone so soon after her piercing.

"Stop looking at me like that!" Lou finally told Nic, exasperated. "You *wanted* to go to the S and M bar!"

"Yeah, and then I wanted to go home!"

"That is exactly what's wrong with us. We don't live life to the fullest! I implore you, Nic, just for this one evening, let's live fully—walk on the wild side!"

Just then, a greasy-haired fifty-something male slipped onto the bar stool beside Lou. "Did I happen to hear correctly? Does one of you ladies want to take a walk on the wild side?"

"Oosh koosh mal," Lou said. What she'd meant to say was, "Not with you, pal," but something weird was going on with her lip. It had swelled up like a balloon.

Attractive, Gigi commented.

Sighing, Lou agreed with Nic's pleadings to go back to the piercing parlor to get the damn thing removed.

She arrived home—dateless and lip-ring-less—to see her parents standing outside Pauline's door with their bags. They were so worried about her, they'd decided to pay her a surprise visit!

When she took her coat off, Estelle stared wide-eyed at

Lou's red bustier and tight black lace skirt—chosen specifically for their trashy S and M qualities—and said, "Honey, I'm not sure clothing like that will help you attract a decent boyfriend!"

12

Yup, it's still December

LOU PLEADED EXHAUSTION and got her parents off to bed fairly swiftly. She herself didn't retire until she'd almost completely maxed out her Visa on a bunch of ugly jewelry some C-starlet was hawking on the Shopping Channel.

She tossed and turned from the bad dreams all night. For a short while in the morning, she had herself convinced that her parents' presence in Pauline's apartment was all just a horrible nightmare.

Until she entered the kitchen, bleary-eyed.

"Fred, there are no eggs or orange juice in her fridge," Estelle's voice boomed.

"Pauline has an orange allergy and she's on a low-cholesterol diet," Lou said testily. "I don't know how severe the allergy is, so I didn't want to bring any oranges in. And I'm not a big egg fan myself."

"Good morning, darling," Estelle said. "An allergy to oranges? I've never heard of such a thing."

"Morning, doll," Fred said. "Estelle, don't worry about it. We'll go out for breakfast. Okay with you, Lou?"

"Fine."

"Good!" said Estelle. "In that case, we'll stay in tonight. I'll make dinner and we'll get caught up."

"Oh—it's really nice of you to offer," Lou said. But she really couldn't handle a cream-of-celery casserole tonight.

Estelle specialized in recipes that featured canned soups. "But you're my guests. How about I cook?"

She finally got them to agree.

During breakfast at the diner across the road, Lou asked her father how his arthritis was and he said it was much better now that he was out of the damp Florida air.

"Maybe we'll move back here," Estelle said contemplatively. "It would be nice for the family to be together again, wouldn't it, Lou?"

Lou mumbled something incoherent after choking on her roll and fled to the bathroom.

Don't be so dramatic, she heard Gigi say. *They're so sweet and you're acting like a teenager.*

Exactly! That's exactly right! I never rebelled, so I'm doing it now. You have to let me work through it.

Truthfully, it's not much of a rebellion, Lou.

You're telling me.

THAT NIGHT she nearly choked to death again when she came out of the kitchen munching on a bread stick and Estelle said, "Lou, darling, this is Michael Sherman, the handsome insurance man I've been telling you about for eons—you know, Kitty Sherman's son?"

"Michael." Lou nodded, then turned a questioning look on her mother.

"Michael's going to be joining us for dinner, dear."

Of course he was.

When they were all seated at the dining room table, Estelle looked excitedly at the steaming casserole dishes. "I can't wait to see what you've made, Lou."

"There's a wine-braised brisket of beef, garlic mashed potatoes and dilled baby carrots."

"I'm impressed," said Fred, who began to heap food on his plate, as did Estelle and Michael.

Poor Michael, Lou thought, studying him. He was the shy and awkward type. Obviously he'd been bamboozled into coming by a couple of old people he couldn't say no to. Lou could tell he was grateful for the food. He probably thought he wouldn't have to talk so much if he just kept eating.

"So, Michael, tell us, how are insurance sales?" Estelle got the ball rolling.

"G-g-good. They're always g-g-good," Michael said. "Insurance is an easy s-s-sell these days. Everybody knows p-p-people who are dying of c-c-cancer."

No one seemed to know quite how to respond to that, so Estelle changed the subject. "Michael, have I told you that Lou used to work for Harvey Gold, the photographer?"

"Y-y-yes, you have, Estelle. S-s-so what do you do now, L-L-Lou?"

"I'm trying to write a feature film."

"O-o-oh." Now it was his turn to have trouble responding. Clearly, he'd never met a capital-I Interesting person before. He stared down at his plate.

Sighing, Lou announced that there was homemade apple pie for dessert.

Just then, there was a commotion at the door and she went to look through the peephole.

The evening just kept getting better and better. It was Pauline, fumbling for her keys.

Lou opened the door and smiled tentatively. "Hey, Pauline."

"Hey, yourself," she said tiredly.

"What's the matter? Why are you back early?"

She came in, put her luggage down, sighed and said, "Oh, it's nothing, really. Three months was just a little too long. I needed a break from all that—togetherness." She sniffed the air. "Mmm. Something smells awesome." She looked at Lou, wide-eyed. "Have you been cooking?"

Lou laughed and hit her arm. "Be quiet. I *can* find my way around a kitchen, you know."

"Oo-oh, I've gotta get me some of that," Pauline said, and headed toward the living-dining room where she stopped when she saw Estelle and Fred—and Michael— staring at her.

Estelle said, "Pauline, darling! You're back early! We were worried about Lou, so we made a trip up, but now that you're back, we'll go straight to a hotel, not to worry."

Pauline recovered instantly. "Estelle, stop! Please don't worry about it. I'm thrilled to see you! Hello, Fred. And—?"

"This is Michael," Estelle said. "His mother is our neighbor in Florida."

"Nice to meet you, Michael."

Estelle got up and headed toward Pauline's bedroom. "I'll just pack our things right up and Fred and I will head over to a hotel. Had we known you were going to come back early—"

"Estelle, please don't even think of moving. I can stay with Rob."

Estelle stopped in her tracks. "Rob?" she said. Estelle loved gossip.

"My boyfriend. The one I was just away with."

"A boyfriend! How wonderful!" She headed back to the table.

Lou grabbed Pauline's arm and pulled her away.

"Hey, I'm hungry."

"The food will still be there in five minutes," Lou said. "Would you all excuse us for a moment? We have to talk privately."

In the bedroom, surrounded by Estelle's powder-blue

polyester safari suits, Lou sighed and said, "Pauline, I'm so sorry."

"Please, Lou, don't even think about it. Estelle and Fred are so sweet. I'm almost mad at myself for coming back early. Estelle would have cleaned like a madwoman before she left and I wouldn't have needed to do anything for another year."

"I'll find them somewhere else to stay."

"Lou, I don't want them in a hotel. I'll go stay with Rob until they're gone."

"They might not be gone so fast. They're talking about moving back. Fred's arthritis acts up in Florida."

"Well, in that case, they'll have to make other arrangements until they find a place. But they're certainly welcome here for a few more days."

"But—you and Rob—is it okay?"

"Why shouldn't it be okay?"

"Well, you came back early. And you said you got tired of all that...togetherness. Did you guys have a fight?"

"*Au contraire,* my dear. He proposed."

"He what! Omigod, Pauline!"

Pauline smiled sadly. "I'm not sure I want to get married."

Lou didn't quite know what to say at that, but she did know that having second thoughts immediately after someone proposed wasn't a good sign.

They sat in silence for a few moments and then the doorbell rang. They looked at each other, got up and walked to the door.

It was Jake.

In black jeans. Looking like a Calvin Klein ad.

"Jake! What are you doing here?" Pauline said, hugging him.

"Hey, cuz. I ran into Rob at the Havajava. He said you

were back. I knew you hadn't planned to come back this early. I just wanted to make sure everything was okay." He looked at Lou. "Hey, Lou."

"Hey, Jake." She tried to keep her voice casual. And not stare at his chest. He was wearing a very close-fitting V-neck top.

He frowned at the noise coming from the dining room table. "Are there people over?"

"Lou's parents," Pauline said.

"Oh! Well, I'll run on home, then."

Lou breathed an inward sigh of relief. She wasn't ready for her parents to meet Jake yet.

Why on earth not? she asked herself a moment later. He wasn't her boyfriend. She was being ridiculous. Anyway, more guests would keep her from having to make conversation with Michael.

"No, stay," she said.

Jake looked at her curiously. So did Pauline, who said, "Yeah, stay. Lou made enough food for an army."

He smiled. "Great. I'll stay."

On the way to the dining room, he whispered, "You were having guests when Pauline showed up?"

She nodded glumly, thinking he was going to let her have it, but he just smiled and whispered sympathetically, "Roaches, mice and now relatives. You're not having a great time of it lately, are you?"

She couldn't help but smile back. He squeezed her arm.

Estelle beamed at them as they entered the dining room. "Hello, girls, and—?"

"My cousin Jake," Pauline said.

"Jake."

"Nice to meet you, Jake," Fred said. "This is Michael."

"Hello, Michael."

"H-h-hello."

"So, you're Lou's parents. I've heard so much about you." Jake pulled up a chair. "Mmm. Something smells delicious. Who made dinner?"

"Lou," Estelle said proudly.

Jake looked at her, brows lifted, as Pauline handed him an extra plate and cutlery, and set another place for herself.

Lou rolled her eyes. "Why is everyone so surprised?"

"Well, Lou, it's not like you regularly host dinner parties or anything," Pauline said.

"I think maybe she should," Jake said after swallowing a forkful of the braised brisket. "Lou, this is amazing. You're a born hostess."

Lou gave him the evil eye. It was one thing for her to enjoy making a meal once in a while. It was quite another for him to imply that she belonged in a kitchen.

Not that cooking in Jake's professional quality kitchen with him sampling her delicacies with his long fingers didn't have a certain fantasy appeal....

Estelle broke in. "So Jake, tell us a little bit about yourself."

"Well, I work for the Havajava Café chain—"

"He owns it," Pauline amended.

"Really! How wonderful!" She furrowed her brow. "A coffee chain. Wait a minute. Lou, didn't you tell me a while back that you had a date with—"

"No," Lou said quickly. She didn't miss Jake's amused look. "Besides the coffee chain, Jake is also a wonderful artist," she added, hoping to throw her mother off the trail.

Now it was Jake's turn to change the topic. He turned to Michael. "So, Michael, what's your bag, as they used to say?"

Michael looked at Jake blankly. "I'm in in-in-insurance." His eyes lit up. "Are y-y-you in the m-m-market?"

Jake grinned. "Already have some, thanks."

"Hey, girl," Lou said in Pauline's direction. "Tell us about your vacation." She hoped Pauline would realize that she wasn't fishing for more details about her and Rob, that she was just making conversation for conversation's sake.

She didn't need to worry.

"Not much to tell," Pauline said blithely. "You know tropical vacations—good weather, nice flowers, sandy beaches."

"Why the early comeback?" Estelle asked.

Lou sighed. There was no point even trying to stop her mother.

"I missed the cold weather."

Fred grimaced. "You can have it. I was gonna give up Florida until I had a day of this. Now I'm thinking I'll probably go back."

Lou gave silent thanks to Mother Nature upon hearing this.

"I love the snow," said Jake after he'd swallowed some garlic mashed potatoes. "Wow, this is truly sensational, Lou."

Lou tried to hide her pleasure, then turned to Estelle and Fred. "Jake has—how do you put it, Jake?—'made friends' with the snow. He skis and snowboards."

Michael looked dreamily into the distance. "I've d-d-dreamed about s-s-skiing."

"You should try it. I promise, after a lesson or two, you'll be hooked," Jake said.

"Maybe you can go with Lou," Estelle said. "She's never been, either."

Lou glared and Jake looked at Estelle, then at Michael, as if he'd just made an important realization.

"Michael, are you a—relative of Lou's?"

"Uh, n-n-no. I'm a f-f-friend of the f-f-family's, I guess you could s-s-say."

"We've known Michael for ages. His parents are our neighbors in Florida. We decided it was finally time for him to meet Lou." Estelle bestowed a pleased smile on Michael.

"I see." Jake carefully wiped his mouth with his napkin. "Well, I've gotta get going. I have to get to work. Goodbye all. Great dinner, Lou." He rose quickly and headed as fast as lightning toward the door.

Not that that wasn't exactly what Lou wanted.

13

Yes, it's still December. It's the climax, okay?

THE GLOVES WERE NOW OFF. If Lou had decided she wanted to date men with steady jobs, after all, there was no way he was going to let some unworthy, brainless insurance salesman land her first. Jake had walked out last night, stunned, but once home, he'd kicked himself for leaving. Now, a day later, he vowed he'd make Lou Bergman realize, once and for all, that they were meant to be....

ESTELLE AND FRED returned to Florida the next morning—possibly traumatized by Lou's hour-long screaming session after Jake and Michael left. She'd let them have it about inviting Michael without her knowledge. Around midday, just after she returned from the airport, Jake showed up on her doorstep in ski attire. Sexy, silvery ski attire. And even sexier three-hundred-dollar wraparound sunglasses. Apparently, he'd realized that Michael Sherman was no competition.

As if, Lou thought, staring. "What happened to yoga?" she asked.

"Still love yoga. But it's winter. Ski season."

He was holding out a bulky plastic bag.

"What's that?" she said suspiciously.

"We're going skiing."

"We can't go skiing. I don't ski. Besides, there's no snow

yet. Ski season doesn't start until after Christmas, I'm sure."

"They've already started making it at a little resort I know of that's perfect for learning at. And I'm going to teach you."

"Jake," Lou sputtered, "I don't even own a pair of ski pants."

He grinned and held out the bag. "You do now. With a matching jacket and toque."

She stared. "I don't believe this."

"C'mon, it'll be fun."

"Fun, right. Hurling myself down a mountain and breaking every bone in my body sounds like a barrel of laughs."

"You'll be fine. It's a great feeling when you meet nature's challenges."

"Uh-huh. That's what all those upper East Siders who climb Mount Everest say. Of course, they couldn't do it without all those Sherpas leading the way, schlepping their stuff."

"Just get dressed, you."

Lou sighed, grabbed the bag, and headed to her room. "Rich people," she muttered. "Next thing, you'll be taking me golfing."

"Love to golf," he called as she slammed her bedroom door. "We'll do it in the spring."

"JUST RELAX," Jake said an hour later at the Pine Valley Ski Resort as he led Lou out of the ski rental shack. Not only was she finding it hard to walk on her ski boots, she was feeling a little sluggish, having almost fallen asleep on the Audi's buttery-soft seat over the course of the drive. "You'll get the hang of it in no time."

"Wipe that smirk off your face," she said, walking gingerly over to a small grade he'd pointed out.

"This isn't a smirk," he said. "It's an expression of pure joy. Watching you enjoy the outdoors is something I never thought I'd see."

"You and me both," she said grimly. "I'm supposed to be a garret-dweller, hunched over my quill. Besides, skiing and golf are too expensive for poor folk."

"Hey, today's on me. I'm here to prove that even rich people hobbies can be fun and interesting. What *is* a garret, anyway?"

"I think it's an attic," she said, recalling a "conversation" she'd had with Gigi.

"Ah. Well, enough stalling, kiddo. Time for your skiing lesson." When they reached the grade, he put down the skis and poles he'd been holding. He gestured for her to place one booted foot onto a ski, then the other, then he snapped the bindings shut and put on his own equipment. "You don't even need your poles for this," he said. "Just bend your knees, lean forward slightly and go. To stop, point your tips, being careful not to cross them."

She was doubtful. "It's nice that you think I can do this, but really, I should probably go home now."

"Just try it. I promise, if you hate it, I'll take you home, okay?"

"Cross your heart?"

"Cross my heart. And look around—there are a lot of beginners here."

Lou took a look. He was right. She was grateful he hadn't taken her to a fancy resort with experienced skiers—the kind she was sure he usually frequented. There did seem to be a lot of kids and novice adults at Pine Valley, which had just been a short drive upstate. She supposed the intimidating skiers were all in Vermont.

A woman about her age with a friendly smile and a not-so-expensive-looking ski suit smiled at Lou as she headed to the rental shack. "Just learning?" she asked.

"Yeah."

"This is only my second time. Never skied a day before last week. Now I'm hooked. You'll love it, you'll see."

"Promise?" Lou said.

She grinned. "I don't give guarantees, but I can tell you I was extremely reluctant and look at me now."

A man following her said, "Extremely reluctant doesn't even describe it! Ten years I've been bugging her to do this. We could have been skiing for a decade!"

"Better late than never," his partner said, winking at Lou. "Good luck."

"You don't want that to happen, do you?" Jake said to Lou when the couple was at the rental shack. "Learn today and we'll have decades of great skiing ahead of us."

She looked at him.

"What?" he said innocently.

She decided to ignore the larger implications of his remark. "Jake, there are two kinds of people in this world. Bookworms and outdoorsy people. In case you haven't noticed, I'm a bookworm."

"Just ski, Lou."

She sighed, closed her eyes, opened them again and went down the grade, angling the tips of her skis together as she reached the bottom.

She made it without falling!

Jake followed. "Great work! How'd it feel?"

"I hate to admit it, but it was—fun!"

"I do believe you're ready for the rope tow, m'dear."

"Bring it on," she said, unexpectedly exhilarated.

They tramped over to the rope tow and Jake demonstrated how to grab on to it with bent knees to get to the top of the hill.

Her ride up the hill went without a hitch and she skied down it—with Jake behind her—with no problem.

"I'm skiing, I'm skiing," she cried when they got to the bottom of the hill.

"You are." He grinned. "You liked that, too, didn't you?"

"Of course I liked it—it was thrilling. That's not to say I'll always like it," she added, trying to sound a little less excited. "It's a novelty today."

"Novelty, schmovelty. You loved it."

She smiled. "Okay, I loved it."

"And you want more, don't you?" He waggled his eyebrows lasciviously.

Lou took a moment to imagine him saying those words under quite different circumstances....

"Sure," she finally said, forcing the fantasy away. "Lead the way."

"That's the spirit. We'll have you doing moguls in no time."

"I wouldn't count on it," Lou said, her eyes widening.

He laughed. "Okay, we'll take it slowly. Now you have to learn how to weave, so when you go down a steeper hill, you'll be able to slow yourself down. I'll show you how on this hill, you'll go down a couple more times, then we'll head over to the lift."

She looked over to the lift. "You mean, you want me to go down—that?"

He grinned. "Trust me, to an experienced skier, that's a tiny hill."

"It's a mountain!"

"Not quite."

He showed her how to weave—she only fell down

once—and she went down the rope tow hill a couple more times.

Walking over to the big hill, he said, "Still having a good time?"

She threw him a sidelong glance. "Don't play Mr. Innocent with me. You know I'm having a good time. That doesn't mean I'm about to become a St. Moritz ski bunny!"

"I wouldn't want you to, Lou." He put a hand on her shoulder to stop her, then he leaned over and kissed her gently on the lips.

She was stunned for a moment. "What was that for?"

He looked at her. "Just a friendly kiss."

Friends don't kiss like that, she thought. *And friends don't want more.*

She tried to regain her equilibrium at the top of the hill. "Are you sure I'm ready for this?" she asked doubtfully.

"As ready as you'll ever be," he said. "And I'll be right beside you."

Despite herself, she liked the sound of that.

It took a while, but she made it down to the bottom of the hill unscathed.

"You made it down the mountain, kiddo!" Jake said when they were at the bottom.

"Ha. Some mountain," she said, feeling a high the likes of which she'd never felt before. "It's a tiny hill!"

"Wanna go again?"

"You better believe it."

They skied for a while longer, then Lou said, "Okay, I think that's enough now. I have a feeling I'm going to be in agony tomorrow."

"You probably will be," Jake said. "You've just used a whole bunch of muscles you're not used to using."

She groaned. "Great. Nice of you to warn me."

He grinned. "Let's turn in your equipment. Then we'll

head home. There's a teahouse-gallery I heard about that I want to stop at on the way."

She didn't think she imagined it when his hand lingered on her foot just a moment too long after he helped pull off her boot at the ski shack. She suddenly decided it probably wasn't such a good idea to cozy up with him at a teahouse. She'd plead exhaustion and beg to go home to bed.

No, not to bed.

Maybe the teahouse was the better option.

She quickly pulled her foot away.

"So, how long have you been skiing?" she asked as she busied herself putting on her street boots. She wobbled a bit when she stood.

"Whoa, slow there. Real footwear is going to feel funny now." He steadied her with a hand. Not what she'd been going for. She didn't want him any closer.

"I said, how long have you been skiing?" she said a little too loudly.

He looked at her, cocking a brow. "I heard you the first time." He withdrew his arm and started to walk over to the desk to return the skis, gesturing with his head for her to follow. "I've been skiing since I was a little kid. My parents loved to ski." He proceeded to pay the clerk for the rental skis, but Lou protested. "You had your own—let me get that."

"No way. I invited you."

She crossed her arms. "Invited?"

"Okay, coerced," he said easily. "Even more reason for me to pay."

An hour later they were sitting across from each other at a small heritage pine table at Tom's Teahouse and Gallery.

"This place is great!" Lou said, looking around wide-eyed. Far from being a cutesy, chotcke-filled tourist trap, Tom's was more like a big-city establishment in the middle of nowhere. The art featured was neither the sappily romantic watercolor variety nor the cloying folksy stuff normally found in countrified establishments. The canvases on the wall were challenging and hard-edged, perfect for the big barnlike room that was thankfully devoid of flowered wallpaper, Muzak and wooden chairs with hearts carved out of the backs.

"Hey there, folks."

A big, bearded man in a plaid shirt had come over to their table.

"This your first visit to Tom's?" he asked.

"It is," Jake said. "I take it you're the owner of this fine establishment?"

"I am, indeed." He extended his hand. "Tom Bryan," he said.

Jake shook his hand warmly. "Jake Roth. And this is Lou Bergman."

Lou took Tom's hand. "Nice to meet you. This is a great place."

"Thank you. You like art?"

Jake grinned. "We like art *and* good hot beverages. I'm incredibly impressed here, Tom. Loose leaf tea and amazing stuff on the walls."

Tom shrugged. "It's hard to make a living from the art alone."

Jake nodded slowly. "It's a terrific idea. I've been to other gallery-cafés, but they're all so—"

Tom laughed. "Chintzy?"

"Yeah, the others I've been to in the country sure are. There are some in the city, but they're just the opposite—so overly citified that they're intimidating."

Tom nodded.

"Is all the art here your own?" Lou asked, curious.

"Not all, but most of it, yeah."

"It's fantastic."

Tom grinned. "Interested in buying something?"

"Can't swing it just now," Lou said ruefully, "but hopefully, one day."

"Where did you study?" Jake asked.

"The Art Institute."

Jake lifted a brow. "No kidding."

"Yeah. But the city wasn't really my bag."

"I almost went to the Institute," Jake said.

"Really?" Lou said, shocked.

Jake smiled. "I thought about it for a while."

"Why didn't you?" Tom asked.

Jake shrugged and smiled. "Other interests took over."

"So you're an artist at heart?" Tom asked.

Jake shook his head. "Nah. I never did get any professional training. I'm a total amateur."

"His stuff is awesome," Lou put in.

"Yeah? Well, if you want to bring a few pieces by, I'll be glad to consider hanging them."

"Jake, that's a great—"

"Thanks for the offer, Tom," Jake interrupted Lou, "but like I said, I'm doing other things now."

"Suit yourself. Myself, I would find it hard to stop. Once an artist, always an artist."

"I haven't really stopped. I dabble here and there. It's my hobby."

Tom seemed to sense that Jake wanted to change the topic. "Right. So you folks been skiing?"

"Yeah," said Jake. "I'd heard about your place, so we made it our business to stop here on the way back from Pine Valley. It's a great location." He looked around. "Busy."

"Always," Tom said. "In the fall, we get everybody

looking at the leaves, in the winter we get the skiers and in the spring and summer, we get the antiquers."

Jake shook his head. "Brilliant."

"Jake has a café in Manhattan," Lou added.

"No kidding! And here I am asking you to bring your stuff here. You hang it there, right?" Tom asked.

Jake laughed, a little nervously, Lou thought. "God, no. Wouldn't dream of it. I'm not as good as you are."

"You are, too," Lou said.

"Think about it, man," Tom said. "Being your own rep—it's the best." He looked around. "Well, I'd better get back to work. Nice meetin' you folks. Come back."

"We will," Jake said.

"Absolutely," Lou echoed. "Next time, I'm buying a painting."

They were quiet for a few moments after Tom left them with a smile and a salute.

"So," Jake said after a while, "you're a skier now."

He was trying to get her off the topic of art. She went along with him.

"I don't know about that," she said. "But I'll give you this—it was a lot of fun. Wow, this tea is really good."

More silence.

"Your parents are cute," Jake said after a few sips of tea.

"Cute—ha! Are you using that as a synonym for annoying?"

"No. For present in your life."

She felt immediately chastised. "You must miss your folks," she said softly.

He looked at her. "I do." He looked out a window into a panoramic vista straight out of an Andrew Wyeth painting. "They were pretty young, just about twenty-ish, when they had me. Forty-ish when they died."

"Tragic," Lou said soberly.

"Yeah." He spoke in a subdued tone. "They were both workaholics. They didn't make time for the things they really wanted to do."

"I guess they thought they'd have time later in life. People don't like to think their time will be up any time soon."

He remained silent, scaring Lou slightly. She'd thought he would spend all their time at the teahouse gloating about her new love of skiing.

"So you see, I have been doing something right," she added, trying to lighten the mood. "I've been making the time to do what I want."

He looked at her. "Maybe you are on to something," he said.

The near victory wasn't as sweet as she'd expected. He was behaving very oddly, and was ominously quiet.

He was equally subdued on their ride back to the city.

When he pulled up in front of her—that is to say, Pauline's—building, he turned to her and said, "Thanks."

"For what?"

"For coming with me today. I had fun."

For some reason, she didn't feel like making a smart retort. "I'm glad."

He looked ahead, distracted.

"Okay, so, 'bye," she said.

"'Bye," was all he said.

She got out of the car and watched him drive off, wondering what the heck had just happened.

Don't worry, he'll be back, Gigi said.

I assure you, I'm not worried. I don't want him back.

Yeah, right.

14

DECEMBER THIRTY-FIRST arrived in a flash. It was Nic's wedding in addition to being New Year's Eve and Lou's turn to watch other grown children deal with family members. Some deep, dark, envious part of her hoped that Nic's family was as crazy as her own.

"Lou, darling, come into the dining room," Nic's eccentric Aunt Ornella sang when Lou showed up. Ornella was a well-known actress who had offered her elegant uptown apartment for the wedding. She was very rarely in New York—was usually away, touring with a stage production or filming out of town. Nic barely knew her and Lou had met her just once. Both had thought it odd that Ornella had offered Nic her house, but Lou had told Nic not to look a gift horse in the mouth.

She'd known from the address—the northeast corner of Fifth and Park—that Ornella's place would be spectacular and she'd been right. Large and airy, with high ceilings and filled with Art Deco furniture, it was exactly the kind of home Lou would have chosen for herself if she'd had tons of money.

Well, her dream home was slightly more modern: stark-white walls instead of ivory, mid-century modern furniture instead of Deco and no carpeting or drapes, just hardwood floors and roman blinds, like the stuff in Jake's pla—

Stop it, she told herself.

Mary, Nic's usually jolly mother, was sitting at the dining room table—makeup central—with pursed lips and a grim look on her face. She was wearing a prim blue mother-of-the-bride dress that was a stark contrast to Ornella's black-and-white Yohji Yamamoto-ish ensemble. Mary's husband Buster stood behind her. A group Lou was sure was Peter's parents and two brothers stood around grinning idiotically, giving Nic's obviously peeved parents puzzled looks every now and then.

"Truly, Ornella, I don't want any makeup on," Mary was saying grimly. "Hello, Lou."

"Well, hi there, you two! Congratulations!" Lou chirped. She walked over to Mary and Buster and gave them close hugs and kisses with one arm while keeping a good grip on her dress with the other. "Where's Nic?"

"Oh, she's around," Mary said. "Oh, is that your dress?" She looked at the dress Lou was carrying on a hanger. "It's beautiful. Ornella, do not come any closer!" In the makeup mirror on the table she'd spied her sister creeping up behind her.

"You heard the woman, Ornella, she doesn't want any makeup on!" Nic's dad Buster echoed.

"Don't be silly, darlings," Ornella cried. "It's a wedding! We have to look *radiant!*"

Just then Nic came into the room, still in jeans, looking near tears. Her sisters Irma and Fiona followed, chasing their six kids—three each—and trying to prevent them from getting into the gargantuan makeup tray that took up most of the dining room table.

"Hey, Lou." She smiled as if nothing was wrong. "Have you met Peter's family?" She took Lou's arm and guided her over to them. "This is Simon and Flossie. And these are Peter's younger brothers, Raymond and Samuel."

"I'm very pleased to meet all of you," Lou said warmly. "Congratulations."

They all smiled back. "Thank you," Simon said.

No one else said anything.

"So, er, isn't this a lovely place for a wedding," Lou said as Nic went off to take care of some catering crisis Mary was having trouble dealing with.

"Yes," Flossie said politely.

"Very nice," Simon said.

She tried again. "And the weather's quite nice today. Not that we need it—it's an indoor wedding, but it makes it nicer for the people driving in."

"Yes," Flossie said.

"It's very nice," Simon said.

"And you're coming from—"

"Greenville," Flossie said.

"Oh, that's not too far..."

"No, not at all," Flossie said.

"I was at an antique show there once. It's lovely."

"We like it," Flossie said.

"It's very nice," Simon said.

"And what do you do out in Greenville?" Lou normally avoided this cocktail-party question, hating that people in New York were judged by what they did as opposed to the kind of people they were. But she was desperate, having already run out of things to talk about.

"Simon has a medical practice in town," Flossie said. "I help out in the office."

Lou vaguely recalled Peter saying he was the son of a country doctor. She turned to Simon. "So you were Peter's hero, I guess."

Simon smiled. "I would have liked him to join my practice, but you know young people today. They have to head out to the big city."

Change the topic, Lou told herself.

She turned to Raymond and Samuel. "And you boys are in school?" They were twins and she guessed they were in secondary school.

"Eleventh grade," Samuel said proudly.

"Great," Lou said. "And are you going to be doctors, too?"

"No way," Samuel said.

"We're gonna open a garage," Raymond said.

Simon looked extremely uncomfortable. Flossie's lips pulled together in a tight line. Lou had no idea what to say next. Thank goodness the first wedding day argument began at that moment....

"Ornella, that's quite enough." They all looked at Mary, who'd spoken louder than Lou would have ever thought her capable. Nic's mother rose and pulled herself up stiffly. Nic put her hands over her eyes. Her sisters stopped their chasing. Peter's family looked on wide-eyed. Even the kids stared.

"Ornella, we are not children anymore. You cannot boss me around. I know you're having great fun trying to take over my daughter's wedding, but—"

"Take over your daughter's wedding?! Is that the thanks I get for offering my *home,* my expertise—for looking after your daughter?"

"Expertise!" Mary snorted. "What expertise? Being crazy?"

"Mother! That's enough—both of you!" Nic walked over to the dining table and thumped it with a fist. "Mother, we wanted the wedding in Manhattan and I took Ornella up on her offer to hold it here. Offering her home was extremely generous. She's saving us a lot of money."

Mary looked at her fingernails.

Nic turned to her aunt. "Ornella, while I appreciate the

use of your home, I *don't* appreciate your forcing makeup on people who don't want it. We are *not* backstage. We are *not* making a feature film here."

Ornella looked a trifle contrite but remained silent.

"Now, if you'll excuse me, I would like some privacy." Nic grabbed Lou by the elbow and muttered, "Come with me."

She led her upstairs to the bedroom, where her wedding dress was hanging on a rack. She motioned for Lou to hang her dress next to it.

"Oh, Nic, it's gorgeous. I can't wait to see it on you," Lou said brightly, trying to lighten the mood. Nic had described the dress to her—a simply cut satin gown with a princess neckline, but this was the first time she'd seen it.

Nic looked at her friend. "Thanks. What's going on with your neck? I thought you didn't like jewelry."

I didn't used to, Lou thought, realizing with horror that her spending had completely spiralled out of control. She fingered the necklace she was wearing. "Oh, this is just some old thing I had lying around. I felt bad about never wearing it." She refrained from telling Nic that she'd become a full-fledged Shopping Channel addict.

There was a knock on the door and she opened it to Pauline.

"Hey, guys! So, it's the big day, Nic! How are you feeling?"

Nic promptly burst into tears.

"Oh, God! What did I say? Honey, I didn't mean anything by it—"

Nic waved one hand and blew her nose with the other. "It's...it's nothing you—" she sobbed, gulped some air, blew again, then continued "—nothing you said. It's—oh, God, guys, I think I'm making a huge mistake!"

Pauline and Lou exchanged glances.

Lou looked back at Nic and chose her next words carefully. "Exactly what do you think you're making a mistake about, sweetie?"

"Everything!" Nic sobbed. Then she began to babble. "Having the wedding here. I wanted Peter to think I was so mature, that I wanted to have the wedding in the place we were going to make our life, but the truth is, I really wanted my wedding in Mayville, at the Inn, and I wanted my mother and I to decide everything together, and I wanted all of my old friends from grade school to watch the ceremony—" She burst into a fresh round of sobs.

Pauline and Lou looked at each other again, then Lou went over to the bed where Nic was sitting and grabbed one of her hands.

"Honey, before you came to Manhattan, did you and your mother make a habit of going shopping together?"

"Well, no," Nic admitted. "She's a little conservative."

"That was my impression." Nic was Gwen Stefani next to her mother, Lou thought. "And did you invite any of your old friends to the wedding?"

"Three," Nic said softly.

"Are any of them coming?"

"Yes, one," she said, sniffling.

"Do you know why the other two aren't coming?"

Nic sniffed again. "One of them is in Australia on business and the other one is looking after her sick mother."

"So there you go. They wouldn't have come to a wedding in Mayville, either."

"I suppose not." Nic blew her nose.

"And if you'd had the wedding up north," Pauline broke in, "wouldn't Ornella have flitted around trying to put makeup on everyone there, too?"

Nic almost giggled through her tears. "Yes."

"I rest my case. Nic, honey, if other people can't be mature enough to refrain from petty arguments on your big day, well—"

"But—" Nic blew her nose again "—there's something else."

"What's that?" Lou asked with some trepidation.

"I think...I think I'm—marrying the wrong person."

Lou hugged her while she sobbed. "Shush, hon, whatever makes you think that?"

"I don't know. He's really sweet and I love him, but—what if there's someone else out there who's *better?*"

A tricky question, indeed, Lou thought. "Nic," she said cautiously, "you told me a couple of times that Peter was your best friend. You found a soul mate, which makes you very lucky." Would *she* ever find a soul mate? The thought flew unbidden into Lou's head. As did the next thought, which was that she already had one...in Jake.

She pushed both thoughts away. A relationship between them would never work. And what on earth was she thinking, talking Nic into getting married? Quickly she added, "But I definitely think you should follow your instincts and of course I fully support whatever you choose to do."

Nic looked at her as though she were from a different planet. "Do you think I don't want to go through with it?" she asked, giggling. "Don't be ridiculous." She wiped her eyes. "Okay, I'm over it now. Let's get dressed, girls. I'm getting married."

And get married she did, hurrying down the aisle with a decidedly grim look on her face, almost clenching her teeth when she said, "I do."

"NICE PLACE, HUH? Sure beats the Havajava," Lou said genially to Lauren after the ceremony. Nic had invited all the Havajava regulars to the wedding. Only Jake was missing.

According to Pauline, he'd gone to Italy for an unspecified period of time. *Of course,* Lou had thought glumly. *Probably to find a supermodel girlfriend and propose to her on bended knee.*

Not that *she* was interested in a proposal from Jake Roth. Ha! Just because they'd shared a few laughs....

"It's a fairly decent building," Lauren sniffed.

"Listen to her. Daddy just cut off her trust fund. She's living in a dump," Zee said. "Face it, honey, you're one of the working poor now."

"Is that true?" Lou asked her, concerned, after studying Zee for a moment, who looked decidedly odd in a suit. Lou doubted Lauren would be able to handle real life. Hell, Lou hadn't been born with a silver spoon in her mouth and *she* couldn't even handle it.

Lauren tossed her golden locks. "He wanted me to give up certain...friends." She glared at Zee. "I'm fine. I'm staying with a friend and looking for a job."

"What will you do?" Lou asked, curiosity overcoming her—about the relationship between Lauren and Zee as well as the poor little rich girl's future plans.

"I have plenty of options," Lauren said breezily. "A friend of a friend has connections at Christie's."

Ah, of course, Lou thought. Well-bred New York blondes always had connections at Christie's.

"Excellent food," Dent commented. Lou looked at him and smiled. She'd never seen the trucker in a suit before, either. He looked even stranger than Zee.

"The smoked salmon is particularly good," Sam said.

"Sam's right," Vanessa said softly. Sam looked at her. She smiled back at him.

"Everybody, this is Max," Ingrid said.

"Hi, Max," they all chorused. Lou studied Max, who looked twenty years younger than Ingrid. Max looked almost exactly like Ted, except his hair was surfer-blond instead of matinee-idol-black.

"You've been flying solo for a while," Lou commented when Max had gone to get some smoked salmon. "Glad to see you're back in form."

"Mmm," Ingrid said, looking at Max. "Ted was kind of a hard act to follow."

Lou lifted her eyebrows. "But didn't you say he got boring when he became a stockbroker?"

Ingrid looked at Lou. "No, I said I dumped him when he became a stockbroker. And you were the one—ironically—who defended him, saying he was still a terrific person and all." She looked at Max again, who was busy charming a waitress at the buffet table. "You know, kiddo, I may have underestimated boring. Boring can be good."

"You think?" Lou asked, following Ingrid's eyes over to Max.

Ingrid looked at her. "I know."

Lou cleared her throat. "Right, well, I should probably go dance."

"With whom?" Ingrid asked pointedly.

Lou knew she was trying to make a point about Jake—that there was no other man for her, et cetera, but she decided to ignore the implication. "With the groom's brothers, Ingrid. You know, it's possible to have a good time at these things without a boyfriend."

Ingrid shrugged. "Is it? I wouldn't know."

Lou wandered into Ornella's spacious living room, where the dancing was taking place to the sounds of a semi-famous jazz trio. True to her word, she danced with both of Peter's brothers, the future garage owners, as well as Nic's father and Peter himself. Then, pooped, she planted herself in a corner with Pauline and Rob, whom she soon realized, were barely talking to each other.

Excusing herself, she introduced herself to Harvey's new videographer, a young, happy-looking thing—a recent graduate, Lou guessed. She was dressed in surprisingly rebellious clothing—a T-shirt with the logo of an alternative rock band on it over a long-sleeved soccer shirt, with a short plaid skirt and Dr. Martens. Her hair was short and platinum blond. She wore bright red lipstick and blue eye shadow.

"Lou! Great to meet you," she exclaimed, pumping Lou's hand enthusiastically. "I've heard so much about you."

"Good things, I hope."

"All good. I'm Rose, by the way."

"Nice to meet you, Rose. So how do you like working for Harvey?"

"Oh, it's great. It's a blast."

Lou raised her brows. "You think making wedding movies is a blast?"

"Well, yeah, didn't you?"

Lou looked at her. "I wanted to work on my own movies."

Rose nodded sagely. "Mmm."

Lou couldn't help asking, "Don't you ever feel like you'd rather do your own stuff?"

Rose paused. "Not really, no."

"You're...happy working for Harvey?"

She shrugged. "Sure. It's fun and it pays the bills."

Why didn't I have that attitude? Lou wondered. Had she been worrying too much about what other people thought of her?

"Well, gotta get back to work," Rose said cheerfully. "See you later."

"Right," Lou said.

Instead of dancing, she stuffed her face at the dinner

buffet—the makeup had been whisked off the dining table before the guests arrived. While she was pigging out on dilled salmon and mixed greens, Nic's father stood and asked for attention.

Buster loosened his lime-green tie and undid the top button of his yellowish-greenish shirt. He also undid the button on his shiny gray suit. He smiled. "The hard part's over now. Might as well get comfortable."

Everyone laughed dutifully.

He turned solemn. "My daughter Nic," he said, "is the most beautiful, talented and downright sweetest girl in the entire hemisphere. And even though Mary and I gave her a little grief about pursuing a career in photography—" everybody laughed again "—because few people in our neck of the woods do that sort of thing, she proved that she could do anything city folk could do."

More laughter.

"And Peter's a terrific guy, an accomplished guy, a successful pediatrician." He bestowed a benevolent glance on Peter. "We're lucky to have him, too."

At this, Peter's family applauded and everyone joined in, some whistling and shouting, "Yeah, Pete!"

"On behalf of Mary and myself, I'd like to thank the out-of-towners for coming." Now it was Buster's turn to laugh. "Which is most of us." He cleared his throat. "But seriously, we appreciate Ornella lending us her lovely home." At this, Mary kept her eyes straight ahead. "I was ordered to keep this short and sweet, so I'll stop there. Please join me now in raising a glass and toasting Nic and Peter."

"To Nic and Peter," everyone cried, holding up their glasses.

"And now, I'd like to call on Peter to say a few words."

Peter headed over to Buster, an ear-to-ear grin on his

face, which made him look even more teddy-bearish than usual, Lou thought. He was perspiring heavily.

"Buster was right," he said fervently, clapping his father-in-law on the back, "I am the luckiest guy in the world. Nic is so sweet, beautiful and talented. No offense, everybody, but I'm looking forward to leaving all of you tonight and beginning the rest of our lives together." Peter raised his glass. "To Nic!" he said, and everyone cried, "To Nic!"

"And now, my beautiful bride—"

Lou saw Nic shake her head frantically and her stomach fell. *Had* her friend just made a terrible mistake?

"Uh—okay, folks, it looks like my gorgeous bride has decided not to give her speech, but instead, let you guys get back to the celebration. I do believe dessert has been set up on the buffet table, so dig in and have a great time."

After the speeches, a few more people filtered in and a cute, harried-looking guy in a conservative suit and glasses sat beside Lou.

"I hope this seat's not taken," he said politely.

"Nope," she said, still studying Nic.

"Steve Simpson," he said, extending a hand. "Ornella's boyfriend's son."

"Oh!" Lou turned to him. "I didn't even meet her boyfriend—your father."

"He's not here. He's an actor, too, and he's currently on tour with a show. It's in Australia now."

"Oh, how exciting! Are you an actor, too?"

He grinned. "Nope. A financial counselor. That was my way of rebelling. Dad was horrified."

Lou laughed. He was a Yuppie, but he had to have some artistic genes in him somewhere, she thought. They chatted some more until Lou excused herself. Much as she liked him, she didn't want to be around him when the clock chimed midnight. She headed to the bathroom. There, at least, she wouldn't have to kiss anybody she didn't want to kiss.

Not that there was anyone in particular she wanted to kiss.

Unfortunately a whole bunch of other females had had the same idea. Ornella's large powder room and the narrow hallway just outside of it were packed.

One of Nic's cousins—a blond chronic giggler whom Lou had met years ago—giggled in the hallway when she saw Lou.

"Dateless, too, huh?" she said, giggling. Lou couldn't help but notice that her glittery, barely there strapless dress was in danger of falling down each time she giggled.

She mustered a smile. "I don't have to kiss you, do I?"

"Eeew, no way!"

A burgundy-haired, jaded-looking teen in a long black dress with batwing sleeves and clunky boots narrowed her eyes as she took a drag on her cigarette and said, "You're Lou, right?"

"Right. And you are—?"

"Pam. A cousin of Peter's. Nic pointed you out. I'm a writer, too."

"Nice to meet you," Lou said, smiling inwardly. Oh, to have the confidence that teenagers had. "What do you write?"

"Angry girl poetry, mostly."

Lou grinned.

Pam took a deep drag on her cigarette. "God, I *hate* New Year's," she said passionately as she exhaled.

"It's a drag when you don't have a boyfriend," the giggler agreed, looking serious for once.

"Damn straight. And don't even get me started on the resolutions."

"Do not go there," said a woman who had, Lou vaguely recalled, once joined her and Nic for a movie. She caught Lou's eye. "Hi, Lou. Raquel North. I'm Nic's neighbor."

"That's right," Lou said. "Nice to see you again."

"So tell us your resolution story, Raquel," the giggler said.

Raquel didn't look as though she needed to make any resolutions. A stunning redhead with a commanding speaking voice, she sighed and said, "Every year I quit smoking."

"Been there, done that," said Pam, inhaling deeply.

"Gimme one of those, would you?" Raquel said.

Pam dug in her bag and tossed her one.

"Thanks."

"It's cookies for me," the giggler said suddenly mournful. "I'm gaining *so* much weight."

"Well, girls, let me tell you a little about what *I've* been trying to accomplish this year." Lou gave a brief account of her bet with Jake and her subsequent failed efforts to remake her life.

There was dead silence when she finished.

The giggler just stared. Finally, Pam said, "Okay, you win the crappiest year prize."

Raquel said, "Hey, look at the bright side. You have nowhere to go but up." She didn't sound convinced.

They heard the countdown from the living room, then the clinking of glasses and wet, sloppy kisses being planted on various lips and cheeks.

"Happy New Year," said Pam glumly.

Lou turned to her. "Give me one of those things," she demanded, even though she'd never really smoked.

"Take it," said Pam over the strains of *Auld Lang Syne*. She tossed one to Lou. "Sounds like you're gonna need it."

It wasn't an auspicious beginning to the new year.

15

JAKE WASN'T HALF SO GLUM. He'd accomplished a great deal since arriving in Italy. He'd completed several paintings and charcoal studies for several more. And he wasn't nearly done yet. It was as if the dam holding in all his creativity had burst the afternoon of his epiphany at Tom's. It had hit him then that he wanted to be doing exactly what Lou was doing—working on his art, putting himself out there. He'd tried to convince himself he'd made the right decisions—that was why he'd made that bet with Lou in the first place. He'd been intent on proving his path was the "right" one. But he realized now that at least some of his choices had been made out of guilt, out of knowing what his dead parents had wanted him to do.

He looked over to the church up the road where bells were ringing. A flushed bride and handsome groom were rushing down the steps.

It was a new year. A time for new dreams.

Did he dare even dream the one he most wanted to come true?

Not until he could go back to Lou with proof that he was capital-I Interesting enough for her.

Until then, he had work to do.

LOU'S ICKY FEELINGS about her increasingly terrifying financial situation were validated when she went on a date of sorts with Steve Simpson. She had only half jokingly suggested to him that she could use his help in the budgeting department when he grabbed a pen out of his shirt pocket and scribbled "Lou's Budget" on the top of a paper napkin at their bistro table. They were at Numbers, a popular place in the financial district with great food and decor but an unfortunately gimmicky premise whereby each item was named after some infamous New York wheeler-dealer—like the Boesky burger. The place was jam-packed and every other customer looked like an investment banker. Steve himself was wearing the requisite striped button-down shirt, with chinos and a sport jacket.

"Okay, what's your weekly income?" he asked her enthusiastically.

"Uh, nothing right now."

He looked at her, surprised. "Nothing?"

"Nothing," she repeated, feeling compelled to add, "I made pretty good money as a videographer with Harvey Gold. I left that job recently to write a screenplay that's being considered, as we speak, actually, by a bunch of producers."

Being considered a piece of crap, no doubt.

Steve brightened. "Really? Wow. That's terrific. I admire artistic types."

"Except your father."

He laughed. "I admire him, too. But I have to admit, his total lack of financial consideration for his family is what made me what I am today."

At least I don't have kids, Lou thought, depressed. *The only future I've screwed up is my own.* She felt the bile rise in her stomach—from panic as well as hunger. She'd been cutting back on groceries, choosing to splurge on glittery jewels to make her feel better instead. At least she'd get a free dinner—and hopefully, some solid financial advice—out of what already promised to be an interminably long evening.

The waitress came to take their orders. Steve got the Boesky burger—"Even though he's a terrible role model," he told Lou—Lou, the Trump T-bone. Since dining at Steakfrites months ago, she'd found herself craving steaks on a regular basis.

When the waitress left, Steve said, "So, anyway, people like my dad, who follow their passions and don't bring in much money sometimes don't realize that they *are* capable of budgeting and saving to make their own lives and those of their loved ones considerably easier."

Lou felt her spirits lift slightly. Steve seemed like a decent guy. And he wanted to make her life easier!

"So what kind of nest egg are we looking at?"

Okay, so maybe the lifting of her spirits had been a bit premature. Lou felt herself redden and suddenly wished they could go back in time. Asking Steve to help her, it was suddenly, glaringly clear, had been a mistake of epic proportions. What had she been thinking? A guy like Steve would consider the sum of money she had left barely enough for one week of groceries.

How had she let it come to this? she wondered. She had never been the type of person who laughed at the prospect of saving for retirement. She had never thought living hand-to-mouth each month was noble. Estelle and Fred had pounded the importance of saving into her head. And look at them now, living proof of their beliefs, able to enjoy life to the utmost during their retirement years. What had made her think she was suited to living the artistic life? And on top of that, she'd been squandering money hand over fist, sacrificing food to buy crap on the Shopping

Channel! It was as if she'd been in a trance for the past few months....

Steve was looking at her expectantly.

"Well, understand, I'm sure something will happen with my screenplay soon." She stalled.

It would be thrown in the garbage. And she'd have to take up cosmetology after she tossed it.

"Uh, okay. So there's...not much left."

"Practically nothing," she admitted.

"Are you planning to get some sort of steady job soon?" he asked.

"Oh, yeah, real soon," she said, which was true.

"Okay, here's what you do. When you have money coming in, you're going to have to divide it into three sections. One section—the largest—will go into your bank account. It's to cover your living costs, which you will figure out by writing every single fixed monthly cost down on paper."

"Every cost—got it."

"You've never done this before?" he added incredulously.

"Nope," she said.

"Not even a less-detailed variation of it?"

"Uh, no."

"So you've never budgeted at all?" Still incredulous.

"Well, I sort of did it in my head, I guess. I knew how much I was making and—"

"That's not budgeting," Steve said sternly. "The whole idea behind writing it all down is to see what you have and what you don't have. People think they can do it in their heads, but they can't. They don't realize how much they're spending."

"Oh. Right. Okay. Go on." She didn't want him to, but there didn't seem to be anything else to say.

He continued, sighing impatiently. Obviously he hadn't counted on her being just like his irresponsible father when he'd asked her out. "Your frivolous purchases—" he looked pointedly at her DKNY jacket "—will come out of this account, too. But from now on you will *severely* limit any purchases that don't cover fixed costs. You will make notes each and every time you take money out of your wallet."

"And the second section," Lou asked, nearly inaudibly, wanting to get her disgraced and humiliated self out of here as soon as possible. "What's it for?"

"It's an emergency fund," Steven said shortly. "People commonly use it for home repairs and such. Not that you'll be buying a home anytime soon."

Ouch.

"The third account is a retirement fund." He looked at her coldly, obviously expecting her to laugh at the prospect of saving for retirement. She didn't. Suddenly she wanted to grow up to be exactly like her mother.

The waitress brought their food and they ate their meal in silence. Steven dropped her off at the apartment without so much as a peck on the cheek.

See what happens with guys who have money? Lou told Gigi mentally once she was in the living room.

Lou, as you've already figured out, Steve Simpson is no Jake.

Well, Jake's gone.

Maybe not.

Which made Lou wonder, despite herself.

"Heard from Jake?" she asked Pauline casually the next morning as they sipped their usuals at the Havajava.

Pauline looked at her. "No, I haven't heard from him. Don't expect to, really."

"Mmm." Lou went back to reading the *Village Voice,* and

pretended that she wasn't disappointed. "There's a lot of interesting stuff on now. Wanna see a drag version of *Hamlet* called *Hamlette*?"

"Pass," Pauline said, peering at her with narrowed eyes.

"How 'bout a reading of *War and Peace*?"

"Isn't that, like, a thousand pages?" Pauline asked.

"They're doing it over three days," Lou explained.

"Right. At the armory. I read about that. And you want to what, camp out there?" Pauline asked. "No thanks."

"C'mon," Lou wheedled. "It'll be fun."

"Sleeping on some hard armory floor to hear fifth-rate actors reading a book I could never manage to get through? Yeah, sounds like a blast."

"Saw it," Zee piped up from the table beside them. "It's pretty neat."

"Don't you dare follow Zee's advice," Lauren said from two tables away, rolling her eyes. "He is *not* a reliable social planner."

"Okay, are you talking about the time we went to—"

"The zoo when you led me to believe we were going to *The Lion King*? Yes, that's exactly what I'm talking about."

Ingrid, behind Pauline and Lou, rolled her eyes and said, "Jeez, why don't you two just sleep together already?"

There was silence.

"No way," Ingrid cried gleefully. "You already have!"

Dent, at the counter, grinned. "I heard about that."

Lauren gasped.

"Don't worry, hon, it was all good," Dent added, still grinning.

"Now wait a minute," Zee said, "I—"

"Hold it!" Lou called. "This was my conversation."

"It always is," Lauren muttered.

Lou looked at her. "What's that supposed to mean?"

"She means," Vanessa muttered into her coffee, "it's always us talking about *your* stuff."

Lou blinked. She didn't know quite what to say to that.

"Your life is good, Lou," Sam said. "Compared to mine, anyway. I guess what we're all trying to say is that we're getting a bit tired of your whining."

"Me? A whiner?" She was as incredulous as Steve had been upon hearing that she'd never budgeted.

"Not an annoying, over-privileged, rich-girl whiner," Ingrid assured her, looking pointedly at Lauren. "Just a typical, near-thirty-something, navel-gazing whiner."

"Huh," Lou said, still shocked.

"It's just a phase," Pauline assured everyone. "She's getting pretty close to figuring stuff out."

"Does that mean she's gonna hit the sack with Jake?" Dent said.

"Dent!" Lou screeched.

He grinned once more.

"C'mon, you know you want to," Ingrid said in a wheedling tone.

"I most certainly do not," she replied huffily. "And if the rest of you don't care to hear me 'whine,' I suggest you don't listen to my conversations."

"I went to one of those poetry readings in a hardware store," Sam said, apropos of nothing. "Didn't understand a word that was said, but it seemed very interesting."

"Evan's Hardware on Eighteenth?" Vanessa ventured.

"Yeah, that's right," Sam said.

"I read my stuff there sometimes," she murmured, lowering her eyes.

"Yeah? No kidding. That's terrific." Sam had genuine admiration in his eyes.

Lauren turned to Ingrid. "I am not an 'annoying, over-privileged, rich-girl whiner,'" she said. "Just because Zee gave me a twist tie ring and I didn't take well to the gesture...." She pulled herself up. "It was *not* cute."

"Aw, it kind of was," Ingrid said, winking at Lou, who thought back to her encounter with Jim, the faux musician. She could easily imagine him pulling a stunt like that.

"Sorry, guys," she said firmly. "I'm with Lauren on this one."

"Well, of course *you* are," Zee said, exasperated.

"What does that mean?" she asked, offended. "I'm nothing like Lauren."

Everyone looked at her.

"What are you talking about?" Lou asked, in shock. "Lauren and I have completely different values."

Everyone smiled indulgently.

"We do," she insisted. "C'mon, I'm completely broke. What have I been talking about this whole time? I can't even afford a ticket to a real play."

Lauren rolled her eyes. "Oh, for God's sake, Lou, just admit it already. You're a poser. It's been almost a year since you vowed to become 'capital-I Interesting' and your life has barely changed."

Lou's eyes widened. It was true, but hearing it from Lauren, of all people, hurt like hell. "How dare y—"

"Would everyone please leave the poor girl alone?" Pauline said admonishingly. When the others returned to their own conversations, she said in a low, soothing tone, "She's just trying to get your goat. Ignore her."

"But you heard her. She said—"

"Forget about it," Pauline commanded. She looked at Lou. "This whole watch-a-three-day-play is some sort of reaction to the date with the über-yuppie, right?"

"Possibly," Lou said, still hurt.

"Okay, come on. Spill. What happened?"

Lou shuddered. "It was horrible. He took me to this place—"

"Lemme guess—Numbers."

"Great place!" Lauren said, still listening.

Pauline turned to her. "I thought I told you to—"

"All right, everybody, lay off poor Lou," Dent murmured.

"Thank you, Dent," Lou said with as much dignity as she could muster. She turned back to Pauline. "How'd you know?"

Pauline smiled. "I dated a guy just like Steve who took me there once. I had the Boesky burger."

"Steve ordered the same thing."

"I heard they're going to start using Kobe beef and charging a hundred bucks for it."

Lou looked at her. "Are you serious?"

"You bet," Lauren said. "It's the best in the world."

Lou glared at her once again. Lauren quickly put her head down and sipped her coffee. Lou turned back to Pauline once more.

"Why would people pay a hundred bucks for a burger?"

"Because this is New York City? Because they can?"

Lou shook her head. "Well, I tried to give him a chance, I really did. And things were going pretty well until he offered to help me out with a budget. Well, I asked him, I guess."

"Uh-oh."

"Uh-oh is right," Lou said with a sigh. "I've never been so humiliated in all my life."

"Lou, you knew it was risky taking time off to work on your screenplay," Pauline said matter-of-factly. "You were willing to take that risk."

"I've started another one, by the way," Lou said, not

wanting her friend to think she'd just been bumming around since she'd sent *Capra Girl* to Paul. And she wasn't even lying. She'd been playing around with a new script, but it hadn't really gone anywhere until after her evening with Steve, which had resulted in the same kind of frenzied writing that long-ago Visa bill had inspired.

"That's great. Listen, you don't have to worry about money, Lou, not as long as you're living with me. You still have a bit left over for spending, right?"

"Yes—barely. But I feel terrible sponging off you—"

"You're not sponging! I'm enjoying your company. It won't be forever. Don't worry, I'll let you know when you start getting on my nerves. So, tell me about the date already."

"As a date he was a washout, but he did give me a couple of good budgeting ideas. Do you split your income into three accounts?"

"I do, but you can't. You have no income. Repeat after me—I am a screenwriter."

Lou sighed. "My new one is still a long way from being finished. And *Capra Girl* isn't going to sell. I would have heard from Paul already."

Despite Pauline's kind offer to continue sponging off her, Lou knew the time had come to at least consider getting some kind of job. She wouldn't even be able to split the cost of groceries with Pauline much longer. Going back to Harvey wasn't an option; Rose seemed perfectly happy there. The time had come to bite the bullet and to consider something like a coffee shop job.

She hesitated before saying, "Maybe you're right. Maybe I should give it longer. But you know, creative people sometimes take no-brainer jobs to make money while they wait for projects to click."

Pauline folded her arms and looked at her. "Lou, you're not seriously considering flipping burgers or something."

"Well, yeah. I should get a job that doesn't require me to think, so I can reserve my brain for writing. Look at Zooey, serving coffee so she can play in her band."

"I thought she was dying to marry Mr. IBM?"

"Well, she's young. She doesn't realize she's got the perfect life."

Pauline lifted a brow. "Café workers lead the perfect life now?"

"As a matter of fact, yes."

Just then, Zooey came over to their table with a spray bottle. "Hey, guys, how goes it?"

"Peachy," Lou said gloomily. "Made any decisions yet?"

Zooey nodded, her eyes twinkling. "I'm going with Taz. I'll tell Jake when he gets back."

"Wow. Are you sure—"

"That's great, Zooey," Pauline said, shooting Lou a look.

"Yeah, great," Ingrid echoed. Everyone else murmured their congratulations.

Lou turned to Ingrid. "How can you encourage this? You followed your dream—"

"Lou, we've been through this," Dent said gently, "It's not her dream."

"Dreams are for chumps," Sam said sadly.

"They aren't," Ingrid said.

"Some of us were really clear on our dreams and made them happen," Dent said.

"Are you saying I didn't *want* to make a success of my pen protector business?" Sam said hotly.

"That's not what I—"

"Maybe you subconsciously sabotaged it," Vanessa said softly.

"Hey! Maybe she's on to something," Zee said. "You've gotta admit, Sam, it would have been a helluva boring life."

"Mr. Excitement himself is talking," Lauren said sarcastically. "You know, this may come as a huge surprise to you, Zee, but not everyone's idea of a great job is delivering packages on a bike."

"Hey, there's a lot more to it than that. It's like being in an urban bike race every day—"

Lauren ignored him. "As for you, Lou, you've gotta stop projecting your stuff on to everybody else," Lauren said.

Everyone looked at her.

She held up a self-help book. They all said, "Ah," and went back to their coffees.

"When do you plan on leaving?" Pauline asked Zooey.

"Not till early summer." She sighed. "I can't wait."

"What about your band?" Lou said.

Zooey waved a hand. "We broke up. And I'm not crazy about solo work. I'll find something else to do."

"But—"

"Let it go, Lou," Vanessa said gently.

"We all have to let stuff go," Sam said, sighing.

Vanessa looked at him shyly and placed a hand on his arm.

He looked at her, surprised, and a wide smile spread across his face.

"Any coffee shop would be glad to have you," Pauline said to Zooey. "We're going to miss you. Your shoes are sure going to be hard to fill."

Maybe I'll fill them, Lou thought glumly. She dismissed the idea instantly. There was no way she could ever work for Jake Roth.

WHEN SHE SAW THE AD for café workers in the next morning's *Times*—an unnamed chain owned by a company called Lara Foods was recruiting in large numbers—she called and arranged an interview for later that same afternoon.

The bored-looking, gum-snapping receptionist at the personnel agency didn't even want to see a résumé, just asked Lou to fill out an application form and inquired about previous café experience.

"When I was a student, I worked at a coffee shop on the NYU campus," Lou said, which was the truth. She hoped the blonde wouldn't look closely enough at her form to realize that it had been many, many moons since she'd been a student.

The blonde sent Lou off to a back room, which was filled with—what else?—a bunch of nose-pierced, high-school dropouts. A slightly older nose-pierced dropout demonstrated various coffee machines and made the group take turns preparing lattés and sodas. Then they got into groups and cleaned the machines.

The head dropout, whose name was Ben, pronounced Lou his star pupil at the end of the session and told her he was giving her a prime posting at the Havajava Café at—

"Wait a minute," she said dumbly, "this is for the Havajava?"

"Well, yeah," said Ben. He looked at her as if she'd just dropped in from another planet.

"But—the interview was with Lara Foods. Doesn't Lara have its own chain of cafes?"

"Uh, yeah. The Havajava Café chain is it."

"But—Lara doesn't own the Havajava chain. Jake Roth owns the Havajava chain."

"Right." He looked at Lou as if she were a kindergartener. "Roth owns Lara Foods."

IT SERVED HER RIGHT for not telling Pauline she was going on the interview, she thought, shivering as she walked home.

Nic was waiting in the lobby of Pauline's apartment.

"Nic! When did you get back?"

Nic ran over to hug Lou—and got her friend's shirt wet because she was crying.

"What's wrong?" Lou asked, panicked. Had Peter turned out to be a psychopath? A gambling addict? A bigamist?

Nic almost laughed. "Relax. I can tell your imagination's running away with you. It's nothing as dramatic as you're thinking. It's just the now-proven fact that I made a mistake."

Lou put her arm around her and led Nic up to the apartment as she sobbed. Once planted on Pauline's couch, Nic sputtered, "I'm so *dumb!* I felt so pressured to get married! I knew I wasn't bone-deep in love with him. *Knew it!* And still I went ahead and did it! Why? *Why?*"

"Aw, Nic, who knows? Sometimes people are okay with companionship. You thought it would be enough. What happened that was so bad, anyway?"

When Nic's sobs subsided, she paused for a moment before saying, "His whole family came on the honeymoon."

Lou stifled the urge to laugh. "Well, you knew they were a close family—"

"Not that close!" Nic said, blowing her nose.

"He didn't even ask you beforehand if it was okay to invite them along?" Lou asked incredulously.

"Not a word."

"Huh." Lou had been prepared to give a speech about trying to work it out, trying to recapture whatever it was that had initially drawn them together. But if the guy had invited his whole family on his honeymoon without even mentioning a word of his plan to his fiancée, he was sure to be a hopeless case.

"Odd," she mused out loud, "since he didn't follow his dad into his medical practice like he wanted him to."

Nic sighed. "That's just it. He can't get over the guilt," she said.

"I thought you liked big, noisy, country families," Lou said.

Nic threw up her hands. "I guess I've become more citified. It seems I'm a full-blown independent career gal. The guy actually wanted me to take a cooking course on my honeymoon!"

Lou thought back to the first time she'd met Peter and Rob. Rob had been proud of his abilities in the kitchen. Peter had happily confessed ignorance....

"I'm sorry," Lou said soberly.

Nic shrugged. "There are worse things, I guess."

They didn't speak for a few minutes. Nic's occasional whimpers punctuated the silence. Lou fed her some leftover matzo ball soup from the deli across the road and, when she finished, Nic blew her nose again and said, "Things are going to be different from now on, Lou. There's no way I'm going to let the search for a man take over my life. I'm a new woman."

"Hear me roar," quoted Lou.

"What?" Nic said, puzzled.

"Old song. Feminist anthem," Lou explained.

"Oh. Well, I do have some great ideas for improving Harvey's business."

"Really?" Lou was shocked. Nic had always done her job well, but had never exhibited any signs of ambition. "What's your plan?"

Nic spoke slowly. "I have to think it all through some more before I talk about it. Maybe I'll take some business courses first, to get me some credibility. Then I'll talk to Harvey."

"Sounds as if you've been doing some soul-searching."

Nic sighed. "It was a long plane ride." She waved a hand. "Enough about me. Tell me what's been going on around here."

By the time Lou finished recounting her tale of the date with Steve Simpson, Nic was in stitches.

"God, Lou, I don't know what I'd do without you."

"I'm so glad you have my misfortunes to cheer you up," Lou said darkly.

"So what are you going to do?"

She sighed. "Well, I'm certainly not going to work at the Havajava."

"Why not?"

Lou shrugged. "I'm just not." She paused. "Where are you going to live?"

Nic seemed to be mustering up her courage for a moment before she said, "Do you think Pauline would mind if I moved in here for a while, too?"

AFTER NIC MOVED IN, Lou had trouble sleeping, and dropped her last few bucks on some particularly ugly Shopping Channel doodads. Pauline caught on and dragged her to a Debtors' Anonymous meeting. Lou tried not to think about how ironic it was that she, the person who had disavowed the life of the sellout, had turned out to be a compulsive shopper.

By the time they got to the church where the meetings were held, there was a sizable crowd sitting on foldout chairs, sipping bitter coffee. Soon, a pleasant-looking woman whom Lou would never in a million years have guessed was addicted to anything more dangerous than bubble gum, walked up to the podium and said, "Hello.

My name is Irene and I'm a compulsive debtor. Welcome to the West Side meeting of Debtors' Anonymous. Shall we recite the serenity prayer?"

After they did so, Irene passed around a photocopied sheet describing the twelve steps used in recovery programs. Some, Lou realized, would be helpful: admitting she'd become powerless over the addiction, making a "searching and fearless moral inventory" of herself—though she sort of thought she'd been doing that—and making amends to people she had harmed.

She turned to Pauline and whispered, "I apologize for sponging off of you."

"No problem," she whispered back. "I like having you around. Just stop throwing your money away on ugly trinkets."

Lou thought about someone else she probably had to make amends to: Jake Roth. Had she been too hard on him? Too insufferably self-righteous? Too stubborn? Was that why he'd finally stopped what had seemed like a determined pursuit of her? She could only hope he'd return to New York soon—preferably without a supermodel wife—so that she could apologize.

Next, Irene handed out a photocopied sheet with the title "Ten Signs of a Compulsive Debtor"—Lou had seven out of ten—and talked about the tools available to members of DA. Apparently something called a "pressure relief group" almost always yielded good results.

After a guest speaker shared her story, there was "sharing" time. After that, Irene passed around a basket for monetary contributions and then she ended the meeting with some brief closing remarks.

Pauline and Lou walked home in silence.

16

Still February

ON VALENTINE'S DAY, Lou decided to treat herself to a spa evening—at home. She was determined to get a grip on her out-of-control spending habits. She changed into flannel pajamas and a terry-cloth bathrobe, applied and removed an oatmeal face mask, painted and repainted her nails an assortment of colors, and made a tropical fruit salad. *Bringing up Baby* was on TV. It wasn't Capra, but Howard Hawks was the next best thing.

She peeked through the peephole when she heard the knock, groaned and quickly ran through a list of options in her head. Nic and Pauline were already gone. Had she not been certain that Jake had heard her approaching footsteps, she would have pretended she wasn't home. She considered saying something like, "I'm just in the middle of something. Could you come back?" but decided she'd come off sounding as though she'd become a lady of the evening to make that extra cash she so desperately needed.

She opened the door.

"Jake, hi. Aren't you supposed to be in Italy?"

He was in jeans again today. She noticed a couple of spatters of paint on them.

Hmm.

He smiled. "I'm back." His eyes flickered over her flannel pajamas and terry-cloth bathrobe. "Hot date?"

She felt her face redden, but tossed her head as if she didn't care a whit that she didn't look like Karolina Kurkova. "Ha, ha. Come on in. Were you looking for Pauline?"

"Yeah. I wasn't sure if she'd be out with Rob or not. I thought she might be feeling bummed."

"Actually, she is out with Rob. I had a heck of a time talking her into going. Lots of pressure on Valentine's Day." She was babbling, but thankfully they had wandered into the kitchen, so she said, "Drink or something?"

"Just some water. Thanks."

Lou poured two Evians, then gestured him into the living room.

"So you think you did Pauline a favor?" Jake asked once he was seated on the couch. She took a chair.

She shrugged. "Who knows? But I don't think Pauline would allow herself to be talked into doing something she didn't want to do."

"You're right about that."

Long, awkward pause.

"So you heard Nic's moved in—"

"I heard Nic's moved in—"

They both laughed.

"Must be getting pretty crowded, huh?"

"Yeah. She's out tonight," Lou said, then added, "I'll be moving soon. Not far from here," she added in answer to his inquiring look.

"Really? Sold that screenplay, did you?"

"Haven't heard anything yet, but I'm going to be getting lots of steady freelance work soon."

"From Harvey?"

She shifted in her chair. "Yeah. I just talked to him. I need to do something for cash and it turns out the new girl wants fewer hours, so it's a good compromise." Thank

God she'd called Harvey even though she hadn't thought there was a chance in hell of anything coming of it. It turned out Rose *was* happy—just more into three-quarter time than full-time.

His eyes twinkled mischievously. "Hmm. An apartment very close to your old one. Working for Harvey..."

"Hey, there are two months left on the bet, Business Boy. But...I did want to talk to you to tell you that I...realize I've been kind of insufferable lately and I'm sorry if I've said anything over the last few months that...hurt you in any way."

He looked closely at her. "Thank you. Apology not necessary, but accepted."

Another long, awkward pause.

He stood. "So, I'll be going, then. Thanks for the drink."

"No problem." She walked him to the hallway, then stood at the front door with him as he opened it to leave.

Once the door was open, he turned around and looked at her. "So, 'bye."

"'Bye."

He didn't move, just kept looking at her.

She looked back.

"Happy Valentine's Day," he whispered, and brushed her ears with his lips before he kissed her cheek lingeringly until she couldn't stand it anymore. She grabbed him around the waist, pulled him closer and kissed him passionately on the mouth.

"Wow," he said in a low voice once they broke apart, breathless. He took his hands, cupped her face and looked into her eyes.

She looked back.

He bent closer.

They kissed again—slower and harder this time.

Lou broke off the kiss and led him over to the living

room couch, where he proceeded to demonstrate exactly what a really perfect Valentine's Day celebration should consist of.

WHEN SHE WOKE UP, he was gone. As if that wasn't bad enough, Paul Jones called that afternoon. He told Lou he thought she was a terrific writer, but he had felt out some producers and nobody wanted to take on *Capra Girl*. He told her to keep at it.

Pauline hugged her tightly when the tears began to fall. "Oh, honey, it's okay to cry. But there are other agents. You can keep trying. Is there anything else bothering you?"

Did she know? Lou wondered. "Isn't that enough?" she said, sniffling.

"Stop," Pauline said gently. "You have to start getting ready, anyway."

They were going to a New York Film Festival benefit at Tranchet, a huge and ultra-hip flower emporium on 59th Street.

"I don't feel much like going anymore," Lou said, wiping her eyes.

"You're going and that's final. It's the best thing you can do. It'll take your mind off of things. Besides, you might meet some producers there, be able to talk up *Capra Girl*."

Lou sighed. "Schmoozing is not my forte. And there's snow on the ground."

"I know. But you can fake it and it's winter. There's going to be snow on the ground for a while."

Not that anyone could tell it was winter at Tranchet, Lou thought a few hours later. "Are flower shops the new restaurants?" she asked Pauline, fingering a neon-yellow cactus gingerly.

"Is that like 'pink is the new black'? I can never keep up

with that stuff. I think I need a drink. What's your poison?"

"Hmm... How 'bout an apple mar—"

"Pauline? Nice to see you."

Pauline air-kissed a Steve Simpson lookalike. "Mark, great to see you, too! Mark West, this is my good friend Lou Bergman. Lou, Mark is an old friend of Jake's as well as his accountant."

Mark smiled. "Friend, yes. Old, no." He looked at Lou a little too closely.

"I'll go get our drinks," Pauline said, ignoring Lou's laser glare.

"Crazy place, huh?" Mark said, smirking.

"Crazy," Lou said.

"So," Mark said, his smile growing smarmier by the moment, "how do you know Pauline and Jake?"

She sighed inwardly. "I used to work with Pauline and we hang out at the Havajava on Fifty-sixth. Jake's office is upstairs."

She instantly wished that she hadn't told him that. She also wished that she hadn't worn a daringly short satin Daryl Kerrigan minidress. It was an old favorite and until Mark had come along, she'd thought it was the perfect choice for this crowd, a mix of arts patrons, filmmakers and students. She hadn't counted on attracting unwanted attention.

"You live on the West Side?"

"Yup."

"Me, too." He was still smirking. "But I plan to make a switch to the upper East soon."

"That so?" Lou said. *Where the hell was Pauline?*

"Yeah. Jake's rolling in dough and I'm pretty much handling all his business these days."

"Mmm," she said, looking around. She was saved by a

black-clad waiter bearing a tray of gorgeous Jacques Tartouffe hors d'oeuvres. She caught his eye and he came over.

"Goat cheese and lamb drizzled with truffle oil in a Peking wrap?" he asked in a bored tone.

"Yes, thanks," Lou said gratefully, grabbing one. Eating and conversing with snobby servers would keep her from having to make conversation with Mark.

"No thanks," Mark said, looking at the lamb wrap suspiciously.

Jake would have at least tried it, Lou found herself thinking.

"Anyway, can you imagine having so much money that you can refuse to use charitable donations as tax write-offs?"

Lou's mouth stopped midchew. "Jake refuses to use charitable donations as tax write-offs?"

He looked at her distastefully. She'd spoken with her mouth full. "Nuts, isn't it? The guy can really be a wacko. It's perfectly legal. But no, Roth says it undermines the spirit of the charitable donation."

Maimonides, Lou thought.

"I try to save him money, but the guy doesn't want to help himself." Mark shrugged. "What are you gonna do? I drove myself nuts about it for a while, then I decided, hey, it's his life. I've advised him to the best of my ability. He doesn't want to listen, it's his problem."

"Right," Lou said slowly.

Mark looked at her impatiently and excused himself.

Pauline came back with their drinks. "Where did Mark go?"

"Away," Lou said vaguely, still thinking about his revelations. Not that Jake's business practices mattered to her. He wasn't the guy for her.

Was he?

"Uh-oh, don't look now," Pauline whispered, "but your ex is approaching."

Lou groaned inwardly. Why was Alan here? she wondered. Surely it wasn't because he was a film aficionado. She supposed it was just another function for him to be seen at.

"Well, look who's here," Alan said once he reached her, sounding as smarmy as Mark.

Had he always greased his hair back George Hamilton-style? Lou wondered. Strange that she didn't remember.

She smiled coolly, trapped. "Hello, Alan."

"Nice haircut. Hey, there, Pauline."

"Hi, Alan." Pauline didn't even bother to smile.

Alan turned back to Lou. "So, how are things?" he asked.

"Great. Couldn't be better."

"Are you still in the apartment?"

"God, no. Not far, though." He didn't have to know she was staying at Pauline's.

"And work is good? Still with Harvey?"

"Yup." *Sort of.* "You?"

"Super. Made a killing on the stock market a while back. I'm spending more time on my investments than on anything else."

"Great." She paused, wondering if he had, in fact, failed spectacularly at work, if the "investment" line was just spin. "Well," she said, "nice seeing you, Alan." *Not.* "I've, um, got to go."

"Oh, well, nice seeing you, Lou," he said. "Call me sometime."

She stared at him, the light dawning. *He wanted her back.* It was the kind of moment women live for.

Lou grinned. "No, thanks." She turned on her heel and walked away.

Pauline followed her to a quiet alcove. "Good one," she said approvingly as she shoved something into the pocket of Lou's minidress.

"What's that?" Lou said.

"It's a check. Nic and I have decided to invest in Lou Bergman, Inc. We want you to keep writing full time. Now that you've stopped spending outrageous amounts on crummy jewelry, we think it's safe to hand over our hard-earned cash. Take it, hon."

Lou's eyes filled. She heard Gigi say, *No woman is a failure who has friends, Lou.*

She put the envelope back in Pauline's hands, threw her arms around her and planted a sloppy kiss on her cheek. "You're a sweetie. And so is Nic. I'm the richest girl in the world. But I don't need this. Keep it. I'm outta here."

"Hey," Pauline called after her. "Where do you think you're going? The speeches haven't even started yet. And don't you want to see what Jacques has come up with for dinner?"

"I've gotta go!"

"Why?"

"To look for your cousin and ask him to marry me."

"Oh. Well, why didn't you say so?"

AS IF IN A DREAM, a vision of Jake in his ski jacket rose up in front of her. He was laughing and talking with...a beautiful woman. Lou pivoted and ran the other way.

"Lou," she heard him call as he ran after her, finally catching up and grabbing her arm. "Where did you come from? Where are you going?"

"I was at Tranchet for a film festival benefit and I was

heading for your apartment." She was fighting back tears. "It's a good thing I saw you here first."

He pierced her with a stare and started to say something, but just then the other woman caught up to them, huffing and puffing. Lou thought it was odd that she'd run after them, under the circumstances. Lou looked more closely at the woman. She wasn't all that beautiful.

Jake sighed. "Lou, it's not what you think. Kimberly, this is Lou Bergman."

Kimberly. They'd been standing in front of the Kimberly Croft Art Gallery.

"A pleasure," Kimberly said, smiling and extending her hand. "Are you an artist, too?"

"Lou's a filmmaker," Jake said.

Kimberly snapped her fingers. "Of course. I recognize her from your work."

"From your work?" Lou repeated.

Kimberly smiled. "Jake's show will be a huge hit." She turned to him. "Show?"

He grinned. "We need to get some coffee and talk."

Minutes later they were at the Havajava—without Kimberly.

"So why didn't you leave a note, or call in the morning?" Lou asked tentatively.

Jake sighed. "I became convinced that you just used me for some Valentine's Day comfort. You've made it pretty clear over the past year that I wasn't capital-I Interesting enough for you." She started to protest, but he lifted a hand. "Anyway, I wanted to have this thing sewn up the next time I saw you." He paused. "I wanted to prove I could be as capital-I Interesting as the next guy."

"Jake, that doesn't matter. I—"

"No, Lou, listen. You inspired me." He leaned forward and grabbed her hands across the table. "So did Tom. That trip to the teahouse clinched it. I realized I'd put myself into a box. I hadn't painted in ages. I called an artist friend whose Italian villa was sitting empty, and asked if I could use it for a while. I painted like crazy." He paused. "You were right about my being afraid to put my work out there. Kimberly's actually an old friend. She wanted to represent me, but I told her I want to turn the Havajava into a gallery-café, like Tom's. She gave me some great advice, and helped me out with display ideas—it won't really be a show, that's just Kimberly talk."

"Jake, that's *so* fabulous!"

He shrugged modestly. "We'll see." He leaned back again and looked at her mischievously. "So, let's talk about you again. You're still working for Harvey—"

"On a freelance basis. For now, anyway."

"And soon you're going to be living in an apartment of your own not far from where you used to live—"

"A low-rise brownstone as opposed to a concrete block—"

"—and it's only a couple of weeks away from our deadline..."

Lou sighed. "What can I say? You were right. My life isn't so bad. It's actually pretty great. I realize that now. I still hope I can write a successful screenplay one day, but in the meantime, making wedding movies isn't so awful."

Jake grinned. "I won't even say I told you so." He sobered. "And like I said, there was an awful lot *I* was wrong about." He placed a hand on hers. "If this is going to happen, we have to be straight with each other—about everything." He paused. "Who the hell is Rona Bernstein?"

Lou laughed. "She's an old friend. In high school, she became a vegan. I thought she was nuts, and stopped being her friend."

Jake's eyebrows flew up. "You stopped being her friend

because she was *different?* Lou, I'm shocked. You should be ashamed of yourself."

Lou glared at him. He grinned widely and placed his other hand over hers. "I'm just teasing. Lou, people change. Look at all the changes *we've* gone through this past year." He motioned to the waitress. "Now that we've cleansed our souls, let's get the hell out of here."

"Oh? Where are we going?"

"To my place." He looked at her deep V-necked dress. It had been a good choice after all, Lou thought. Jake's eyes were positively feral-looking. "For dessert," he said.

17

The rest of February...and a fast forward to the following September

IT WAS THE VERY DAY after Lou practically admitted to Jake that he'd won the bet when the phone call came.

Lou didn't suspect it would be a life-changing call, since it was just Harvey. He asked her if she'd mind coming into the office to talk. She didn't really want to. She was still blissed out from the night before, but besides that, it was Sunday and she and Jake were reading the newspaper over bagels and coffee. But something she'd never heard in Harvey's voice made her agree to meet with him. She suspected he'd fired Rose for some reason and was desperate to get Lou back full-time.

When she arrived at his office, his chair was swiveled around so he was facing the wall behind his desk.

Harvey had always had a lot of what Lou thought of as the life force in him. He was a man of large appetites, with a commanding bulk to him and an equally commanding presence. Ever since she'd known him, he'd worn his thick silver hair on the longish side, like a mane. She couldn't help but notice that his hair had grown thinner, as had his shoulders. The latter may well have been the work of his wife Elise and daughter Deborah, who were forever on him about eating better, but somehow, Lou thought otherwise. His posture indicated defeat, somehow.

He was looking up at his framed university degree. "Sit down, Lou," he said without turning around.

She walked to the chair in front of his desk. He seemed unnaturally quiet.

"Did you know I have a film degree, Lou?"

"Yeah, Harvey, I did know that."

"The last real film I made was in film school."

She remained silent.

He swiveled around in his chair. "My best friend died last night. Massive heart attack."

"Oh, Harvey—I'm so sorry. Was it Sid—the carpet guy?"

"Yeah, it was Sid the carpet guy. Only Sid wasn't just a carpet guy. He was a writer who never got his book written." Harvey leaned back in his chair. "We went to high school together. Had a blast. Sid was always scribbling stuff—funny poems about our classmates and such. Wrote the scripts for all the school plays—our school always put on original plays. Everyone thought he'd go on to fame and fortune."

"So what happened?" Lou asked, curious.

Harvey shrugged. "Life happened. His father, who started the carpet business, got sick and nearly lost the business. His mother couldn't manage it—she had four kids younger than Sid. He quit school and took over."

"He didn't ever write on the side? Lots of people do that."

Harvey shrugged again. "I don't think he thought there was any point. People do that with the intention of eventually making it a full-time career—they just keep their other jobs while they have to until they get established. But Sid had his mother and younger sisters and brothers to support. His father had just scraped by in the business— there wasn't much in the way of savings or insurance.

Anyway, soon he met Eloise, married young and had his own family." He paused. "Eloise tried to get him to write every now and then—she'd heard about his high school stuff—but he always refused, said that was all behind him. I think she felt guilty about it. Anyway, last night she told me I'd better make my film before it was too late."

"You—have a film you want to make?"

"I've had a screenplay in my dresser drawer for about twenty-five years, but I reread it last night and it's a piece of junk." He shrugged. "That's okay. I'm not really interested at this point in being crapped on by a bunch of number guys."

"So, what do you want to do, exactly?"

He leaned forward. "I want to *be* one of the number guys. I'm planning to bring in Nic and Pauline as partners here—maybe sell altogether. I've made enough money. I'm gonna go out on my own as a producer."

Lou suddenly realized why Harvey had called her in and, in anticipation, she felt her heart soar.

"Pauline's been kind of antsy lately. She's a smart lady. And Nic, all of a sudden, wants to focus on her career. They'll take good care of the business. I barely do anything anymore and I'm bored to tears feeding the stray herons lox and bagels in Fort Lauderdale. I want to spend the rest of my life producing interesting, quality films." He leaned back again. "Word has it that you have a pretty good screenplay kicking around. Any chance you'll let me have a shot at producing it?"

"MAKES FOR A GREAT STORY," Pauline commented seven months later as she read the interview in the *Village Voice* in which Lou explained how her good fortune had come about. It was a gorgeous fall day, and Pauline and Nic were curled up on Jake and Lou's living room couch, sipping coffee.

"You can't possibly expect me to go back to my own apartment after this," Nic said dreamily, leaning back and taking in the magazine-layout surroundings of the apartment that was formerly Jake's, and that now belonged to Lou, as well. "This is too fabulous."

"Don't get used to it," Lou said teasingly. "The only reason I've invited you guys around so much is that I'm determined to finish off those ten pounds of coffee sometime this year."

"This is the end of it, I hope," Pauline said, sniffing her cup.

"It is, and yes, it's still good. Trust me, I wouldn't poison you just when you and Nic are taking HNP Photography to new heights."

Pauline grinned. "Indeed we are."

"I remember Jake telling me Pauline's been saving since kindergarten, but I've been meaning to ask for ages, Nic, how did you swing buying it?" Lou was curious.

"I'm a country girl, remember?" Nic said. "While you guys were out clubbing it in your teens, blowing money on outrageous covers and fancy duds—"

"Not me," Pauline said.

"Okay, not you. I was square dancing at the Legion Hall."

"You made up for it later on," Lou said, grinning. "Remember that S and M place I dragged you to?"

"Don't remind me," Nic said, rolling her eyes.

"Hello? What's this?" Pauline said. "You guys went to an S and M place and didn't take me?"

"You were on vacation at the time. I'm sure the sexual adventures you were having with Rob were infinitely more interesting than the tame displays we saw that night," Nic said, laughing.

"There were no adventures. It was a disaster, remember?"

"Well, there were no displays, either," Nic groused.

"Which was just fine with you, if I recall," Lou said.

Nic grinned. "I've become much more adventurous since then."

"Not to mention ambitious," Lou said. "I hear you two are giving Martha Stewart a run for her money, building a regular wedding empire."

"Not quite," Nic said modestly. "But HNP Photography *is* branching out into some cool new areas. Hey, guess what? Jacques Tartouffe is subletting part of our new space!"

"He of the lamb and goat cheese hors d'oeuvres?" Lou said, her eyes wide.

"The very same."

Lou shook her head. "And you've got how many photographers and videographers on staff now?"

"Two of each in-house, two freelance photographers and two freelance videographers—you and Rose," Nic answered. "And that may not even be enough. I've been doing quite a few nights myself lately."

"Hire someone else. You should work a little less and start having a little fun," commanded Lou.

"Where do you want me to go? Singles bars? What for?" Nic asked scornfully. She was blissfully happy on her own. Pauline and Rob, on the other hand, were slowly edging toward some kind of permanent arrangement. Lou and Jake had tied the knot in an intimate ceremony two days after Harvey had proposed financing *Capra Girl.*

"No candidates?" Lou asked.

Nic wrinkled her nose. "Not interested in finding any."

"Maybe some actor at my premiere will sweep you off your feet."

"Please, they're all of Perry and Paul's ilk. Didn't you notice at the party?"

Paul had happily agreed to be Lou's agent once Harvey had agreed to produce *Capra Girl*. Lou's film had remained a relatively low-budget production, but by some miracle, the film had been selected as one of the galas at the upcoming Soho Film Festival on the basis of a quickly shot and hastily put-together rough cut—Paul's brilliant idea. When he'd gotten word of its inclusion in the festival, he and Perry had organized a huge soirée at their downtown loft. It turned out the old friends were lovers!

"I loved the look on your face when you found out that Perry was an estate lawyer." Pauline chuckled.

Lou rolled her eyes. "Can you believe it? All that time I thought he was so creative, so cool."

"He *is* creative and cool," Nic insisted.

"You're right," Lou said. "Among other things, I've learned that I can't judge people by their jobs."

"Although you'd think he would have chosen an area of law that's a bit more—social," Pauline said. "He sure seems to love a good party."

"That's probably because he works with dead people all day," Lou said.

"Who can't very well be capital-I Interesting," Pauline said. "As opposed to yourself. You are now officially a capital-I Interesting person."

"Mmm. But I've decided that it's okay to retain some elements of my former life as a materialistic conformist—the uptown, pest-free apartment I have to come home to, for example."

Nic cleared her throat. "I seem to recall a good friend of yours reminding you of the virtues of living uptown...."

"You did, indeed, Nic. But I had to figure it out for myself."

"Just as your hubby had to figure out that he could be an artist *and* a businessman."

Lou grinned. "Have you seen the stuff he hung at the Havajava last week?"

"Of course," Nic said. "Two of the photographs are mine."

"You're amazing, girl," Lou said admiringly. "I don't know where you find the time to do it all."

"The same place you find the time to make wedding videos for us *and* write brilliant screenplays."

Lou leaned back in her chair and contemplated her existence for a moment. "I'm okay with making wedding videos now. It gives me a nice break from the screenplays. It gets me out there, talking to people. Here's a newsflash—I wasn't crazy about sitting at my desk and writing all day. I really owe you guys for giving me the work—besides which, we need the dough. Maybe Jake will be able to sell the Havajava one day, but in the meantime, he's gotta keep hawking coffee to keep us in the style to which we've become accustomed."

Nic grinned. "He wasn't as rich as you thought, huh?"

"Not even close," Lou said, looking around the apartment and shaking her head in disbelief. "Can you believe he made all the furniture and did all the art himself?"

"I can," Pauline said wryly. "I helped him. But I seriously doubt he'll have to hawk coffee or be a weekend do-it-yourselfer much longer—his stuff is fabulous. And despite your sudden love of the wedding biz, I suspect you'll be out of it pretty soon. *Capra Girl* is the talk of New York."

Lou smiled modestly. "It's all talk, so far. My life hasn't changed all that much. Jake really didn't have to pay up, as far as I was concerned." She threw up her hands. "Here I am living on the upper West Side, making wedding videos and realizing my life is pretty terrific."

"Nevertheless, you *are* a screenwriter who's getting a lot of buzz," Pauline persisted.

"It's a great movie," Nic said firmly.

"Harvey and Skye did a terrific job with it," Lou said. "Skye's a huge talent, don't you think?" Skye Blue was the young director who'd taken *Capra Girl* to previously unimagined heights of quirkiness. Lou had approached Harvey about directing it herself—she had gone to film school, after all—but he'd felt more comfortable going with Skye on this one. She'd already proved herself with a couple of quirky, modestly successful features. He'd promised Lou that if she managed to pound out two more successful screenplays, she could direct the third. She'd happily agreed to the deal.

"She *is* a huge talent, but she had a great script to work with," Pauline pointed out.

"Speaking of scripts," Lou said, "Barbara Laver is writing one."

"No way! That's too delicious. How do you know?" Nic asked.

"She came to me for advice."

"Grovelling!" Pauline said triumphantly. "Did you love it?"

Lou sighed. "It was weird. I felt bad for her. Apparently, Jack had been cheating on her for ages and on top of that, he wiped her out financially. And then she was fired."

"She's a big girl. She earned plenty of money over the years. She should have watched over it herself," Nic said firmly.

"Look who's talking, Miss Only-Recently-Converted-to-Independence. How was she to know that Jack was a lying, cheating, stealing scumbag?" Pauline turned back to Lou. "So what's her script about?"

"It's a thinly veiled account of her recent experiences. Not exactly a tell-all, since it's fictionalized. It's got a surprising depth to it, some real heft. I'm helping her shape it a bit."

"You're *helping* her?"

Lou shrugged. "People change. I'm more confident, she's been humbled. We're getting to be friends."

"That's great, Lou," Nic said, "but I still can't believe she asked for your help after treating you so badly." Nic shook her head. "God, the chutzpah some people have."

Lou and Pauline looked at her.

"Did you just say 'chutzpah'?" Lou asked.

Nic knit her brow. "Yeah, so what?"

"You know chutzpah is a Yiddish word."

"Yeah, I know. So?"

Pauline grinned and slapped her on the back. "Congratulations, kid. You are officially a New Yorker."

Nic rolled her eyes. "Hey, did you guys hear about Zee and Lauren?" she said suddenly.

Pauline and Lou looked at her.

"What about them?" Lou said.

Nic grinned, savoring the moment. "Last I heard, they were engaged."

"No!" Lou gasped.

"Yes," Nic said triumphantly. "And that's not all."

"Is this how you spend your evenings now? When you're not photographing weddings, that is. Catching up on gossip?" Pauline said in a stern tone.

"Yup." Her grin widened. "Ingrid and Dent."

"Okay, you're just toying with me now," Lou said flatly, crossing her arms. "What is this, *Seven Brides for Seven*

Brothers? Anyway, that's just completely unbelievable. No way is that happening."

Nic held up one hand and placed the other on her heart. "Honest to God, it's true."

"She did say a while back that she was tired of actors," Pauline reminded Lou.

Lou wrinkled her brows. "And she did tell me once that boring was good."

"I don't know if you can call a trucker boring," Nic mused.

"Ah, so you're attracted to truckers, are you?" Pauline said teasingly.

"There is something about them. They have those moustaches, and wear Levi's, and there's all that cool lingo."

"From doctors to truckers. You really have changed," Lou said, grinning.

Nic ignored her. "There's more."

"I'm with Lou. This is too crazy," Pauline pronounced.

Nic smiled devilishly. "You know what I'm going to tell you, don't you?"

"No way, Nic," Lou said. "You are *not* going to sit there and tell us that Sam and Vanessa are a couple...."

"I surely am."

"You're kidding!" Lou screeched.

"Swear on a stack of bibles. Come on, you guys, that was the most obvious one. They've been making goo-goo eyes at each other for months."

"I never noticed," Lou said wonderingly. "Wow, Lauren was right. I really was self-absorbed."

"Everyone's entitled to a little panic the year before thirty," Pauline said, patting her friend's arm. "We forgive you."

"Don't you think they're an interesting couple?" Nic asked.

Lou lifted a brow. "Interesting? Sam? I don't think so. Vanessa, maybe. Sam's nice and all, but it won't last. They don't have anything in common."

"Are you joking?" Nic said incredulously. "They're exactly the same. Shy and creative. You've missed another development. Sam's started to sculpt."

"No," Lou exclaimed. She couldn't believe what she was hearing. Then again, the way her life had gone in the past few months, she knew anything was possible.

"That's why his pocket protector business never took off," Nic continued. "He's an artist at heart. It just took him a while to see his true destiny—like you."

"Yeah," Jake said as he entered the room holding a cake with a single lit sparkler aloft. "And the guy actually has some talent—like you." He pecked Lou affectionately on the cheek as he set the cake down. "He showed me his portfolio the other day. I'm thinking of displaying a couple of his pieces at the Havajava." He dimmed the lights. "Happy thirty-and-a-half, sweetheart."

"Aw, you didn't have to do that, sweetie."

"I know, but I figured baking a big mocha cake would get rid of some of the bet coffee, once and for all. Now make a wish."

Lou shrugged. "I don't have anything left to wish for."

"Sure you do," Pauline said. "Not having to make wedding videos for us."

"But I told you, I don't mind making wedding videos anymore—"

"Yeah, right. Bull. Once you direct that third screenplay, you're a goner."

Lou smiled and shrugged. "Okay, maybe." She closed her eyes and blew out the candle.

"What did you wish for?" Nic asked excitedly, still a country innocent at heart.

"Good presents. Come on now. I saw how bulky those tote bags were. Hand 'em over."

"Mine's coming later," Jake said, waggling his eyebrows lasciviously.

Pauline pulled a package out of her tote bag with the Peach Berserk Cocktails logo on it. It was a Canadian label Lou adored.

"Pauline, you didn't," Lou gasped. "It's not even a real birthday!"

"I did. And it's not just for your dumb half-birthday—it's for the film festival."

Lou ripped the box open. It was a skirt she had admired with the words "I really want to direct" silkscreened all over it. "Oh my God—I love it!" she screeched. "I'm going to wear it to the premiere!" She reached over to kiss her best pal. "You're a doll."

Nic handed her another box with a Fresh Baked Goods logo on it. It was another label Lou loved. She tore open the wrapping. It was a fur-collared sweater that matched the skirt. "Oh, Nic, it's awesome." She reached over to kiss her other best pal.

"Were they good enough?" Pauline asked.

"Better than good."

"You do realize they're bribes," Nic said. "Promise you won't ever forget us?"

"What is *with* you guys?"

"I'll bet you ten pounds of coffee," Jake broke in, "that Lou won't ever forget either of you."

"You bet I won't," Lou said fervently. "Why would I want to forget you?" She leaned back and sighed contentedly. "You know, I really do have a wonderful life."

You sure do, kiddo, Capra Girl echoed.

And Lou never heard from her again.

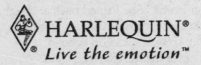

If you enjoyed what you just read,
then we've got an offer you can't resist!

Take 2 bestselling
love stories FREE!
Plus get a FREE surprise gift!

Clip this page and mail it to Harlequin Reader Service®

IN U.S.A.
3010 Walden Ave.
P.O. Box 1867
Buffalo, N.Y. 14240-1867

IN CANADA
P.O. Box 609
Fort Erie, Ontario
L2A 5X3

YES! Please send me 2 free Harlequin Flipside™ novels and my free surprise gift. After receiving them, if I don't wish to receive anymore, I can return the shipping statement marked cancel. If I don't cancel, I will receive 2 brand-new novels every month, before they're available in stores! In the U.S.A., bill me at the bargain price of $4.24 plus 50¢ shipping & handling per book and applicable sales tax, if any*. In Canada, bill me at the bargain price of $4.94 plus 50¢ shipping & handling per book and applicable taxes**. That's the complete price—what a great deal! I understand that accepting the 2 free books and gift places me under no obligation ever to buy any books. I can always return a shipment and cancel at any time. Even if I never buy another book from Harlequin, the 2 free books and gift are mine to keep forever.

151 HDN DU7R
351 HDN DU7S

Name	(PLEASE PRINT)
Address	Apt.#
City	State/Prov. Zip/Postal Code

* Terms and prices subject to change without notice. Sales tax applicable in N.Y.
** Canadian residents will be charged applicable provincial taxes and GST.
   All orders subject to approval. Offer limited to one per household and not valid to
   current Harlequin Flipside™ subscribers.
   ® and ™ are registered trademarks of Harlequin Enterprises Limited.   FLIPS03

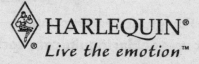

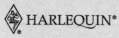

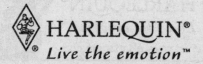

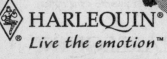